Cosmic
Wonder

.ll.

Cosmic Wonder

OUR PLACE IN THE EPIC STORY OF THE UNIVERSE

WRITTEN & ILLUSTRATED BY

NATHAN HELLNER-MESTELMAN

Edited by Leila Marshy, Jennifer McMorran
Proofread by Edward He, Christina Soubassakou
Cover design: Debbie Geltner
Cover image and interior illustrations: Nathan Hellner-Mestelman
Author photo: Park Photo Studio by Matt Kim

Library and Archives Canada Cataloguing in Publication
Title: Cosmic wonder : our place in the epic story of the universe /
written & illustrated by Nathan Hellner-Mestelman.
Names: Hellner-Mestelman, Nathan, author.
Description: Includes bibliographical references.
Identifiers: Canadiana (print) 20230562078 | Canadiana (ebook) 20230566367 |
ISBN 9781773901596 (softcover) | ISBN 9781773901602 (EPUB) |
ISBN 9781773901619 (PDF)
Subjects: LCSH: Cosmology—Juvenile literature.
Classification: LCC QB983 .H45 2024 | DDC j523.1—dc23

Printed and bound in Canada.

The publisher gratefully acknowledges the support of the Government of
Canada through the Canada Council for the Arts, the Canada Book Fund,
and of the Government of Quebec through the Société de développement
des entreprises culturelles (SODEC).

Linda Leith Publishing
Montreal
www.lindaleith.com

TABLE OF CONTENTS

DISCLAIMER

Where are we in the universe? Where do we come from? Where are we going? What are we made of? Are we alone in the cosmos? Would you like to know the answers to those questions? Because if you would, you should stop reading. This book is not supposed to make sense—not because the author is a bad writer, but simply because the universe is too awesomely vast to be understood. We can stare at huge numbers and look at neat facts, but if anything in this book feels easily understandable, it probably isn't being read correctly. The cosmos has no obligation to make sense to us. The author claims no responsibility for any existential crises resulting from this book's contents.

PREFACE

Hey, thanks for picking up my book!

Have you ever stared up at the night sky for so long that your neck hurt for a whole week afterward? Maybe you were so fixated by the stars that your partner turned to you and said, "Hey, my eyes are down *here*, you know." Perhaps you've watched the sunrise and felt a mild sense of vertigo when you realized that the Sun was not actually rising—it was *you* who was being turned toward the Sun on a huge rotating ball. Maybe someone asked you what was up, and you struggled to find an answer, so you pointed at the sky instead.

If you've experienced any of those, I can relate.

I'm Nathan Hellner-Mestelman, a passionate writer and advocate of science, art, and futurism. I can't remember when I first became fascinated by the cosmos, but whenever it began, I knew I was obsessed. For as long as I can remember, learning about our place in the universe has been a lifelong passion of mine.

Growing up, the only two items I wanted were a microscope and a telescope—one for the unthinkably small, the other for the unimaginably large. Over the years, I used both of them countless times to see what human eyes couldn't possibly show me: the worlds beyond. Millions of tiny bacteria, plant cells, and rotifers swam in a single drop of pond water. Cells divided, grew, consumed each other, broke down, and repaired themselves in a vast, teeming ecosystem that was too small for human eyes to see. A tiny patch of the night sky contained millions of stars, nebulae, and galaxies. The planets, which looked like tiny dots to the unaided eye, became huge and detailed globes, swirling with clouds and weather, orbited by their own moons.

When I was 10, I took the opportunity to join the Royal Astronomical Society of Canada, in which I was surrounded by a group of people who truly loved looking to the stars. Quite literally, it opened my eyes to the universe. As I spent summer Saturday evenings at the Dominion Astrophysical Observatory, I began to appreciate how small we are in the universe. Even as our planet rushed through space at 600 kilometers per second, the stars appeared to stand still. When I looked up at the Milky Way, I realized that I wasn't looking up at all; I was looking straight ahead in our galaxy. The only thing that told me I was looking up was the little tug of gravity keeping my feet rooted to the Earth's surface. In reality, I was being pinned at a 90° angle relative to our galaxy. I was a speck of dust, stuck to the edge of a cliff. That summer changed my perspective forever.

It taught me to never take anything for granted—not even the simple notion of *up* and *down*. It encouraged me to see a view of the world that was less clouded by artificial human creations like money and borders. As I learned theories about the origin—and the catastrophic ending—of our planet and our universe, it let me appreciate how fortunate we are to be alive in the first place. The perspective the universe gives us, in my humble opinion, is one of the greatest experiences we can have.

Granted, not everyone is obsessed with random fun facts. However, as soon as we can feel connected to the bigger picture, it changes our perspective about *who* we are, not just *where* we are. In the past, when classmates have told me that they hate science, it's occurred to me that they probably didn't hate science itself, just the abstractness of the way it was taught. As soon as we bring ourselves into the picture—and we stop throwing out academic facts to memorize and repeat back—it becomes a method of learning more about ourselves as well as learning more about the world. That is a teaching style I have learned and loved for many years.

On January 20, 2019, the Moon moved right into the shadow of our planet, treating us to a total lunar eclipse. That night, I'd set up my telescope to watch the eclipse with some friends and family. I had already seen several lunar eclipses—except, about halfway through this eclipse, one of my friends shouted, "Whoa! Did you see that!?"

Of course not. I was eating a cookie at the time.

The next day, we checked the news, and it turned out that a small asteroid had smashed into the surface of the Moon during the eclipse. It produced a faint flash that was spotted by cameras and observers around the world—all of whom just happened to be looking in the right place at the right time. Not long after, scientists used the Moon Impacts Detection and Analysis System to determine that the asteroid was about twice as wide as a basketball. It slammed into the Moon at 17 kilometers per second—almost fifty times faster than a supersonic jet—and it blew up a crater as wide as a house. All anyone saw, here on Earth, was a tiny flash that was quicker than the blink of an eye.

The impact seemed so small, it was almost worth a laugh, but then I considered: if that asteroid had smashed into a city here on Earth, it likely would have levelled a building, destroyed dozens of houses, and made global news headlines. Fires would have started, medical aid would have been urgently needed, and people would have been evacuated. The damage would have taken months to repair. The tragedy would have been remembered forever.

But no, instead it hit the Moon.

And because it hit the Moon, the only reason we knew about it was because it happened during a lunar eclipse and people had pointed their telescopes at the sky. Some of them were lucky enough to catch it on video, but it was also easy enough to miss just by sitting down to eat a cookie. But it instilled a cosmic awareness that these collisions are happening all the time, on worlds far from here, without us ever noticing. Huge rocks are hurtling their way across the cosmos, exploding like bombs on distant planets, and we are completely unaware that it's happening. Take a nice long breath of air—three seconds in, three seconds out. In the time it took you to breathe, almost ten thousand stars blew up across the universe, vaporizing entire planets into nothing but hot gas and plasma. And here we are, eating our cookies here on Earth.

To me, learning about our place in universe hasn't just been a nerdy obsession; it's been a way of letting go of the artificial structure of society. On February 24, 2022, I was sitting in English class when the news reached us that Russian forces had invaded Ukraine. I can't remember quite what else happened that morning, other than feeling a deep frustration with the fact that a border—an imaginary human invention—had led to the actual loss of human life. Just over a year later, on March 13, 2023, the Willow project was approved to begin drilling for oil in Alaska. It amazed me how money—another imaginary human invention—had pulled us away from the climate crisis at hand. The fact that oil is cheaper to mine and sell, once again, caused it to be favoured over greener energy.

The reason that I chose to write a book about our place in the universe, in a simple sense, is to share a cosmic perspective. It is my hope that, in reading this, you'll feel connected to every other human being on this planet—ignoring money, national borders, races, religions, and ideologies. Our world is a divided place, but we're all living under the same sky. We all come from the same cosmos.

Keep looking up.

PART 1
THE DEEP DIVE

AN INTRODUCTION TO OUR UNIVERSE

We used to think the Earth was the divine centre of the universe. It turned out to be a speck of dust orbiting a massive burning star. That star turned out to be a speck of dust among hundreds of billions of stars in our galaxy, and that galaxy turned out to be a speck of dust among two trillion galaxies in the observable universe. Our whole universe might be a speck of dust too, but we can't know for sure.

Humanity, which for most of our history seemed so special and superior to all other life forms, turned out to have the same soupy origin as every one of the 8.7 million other species on our planet: whether in the wet oceans, the smoky sky, or rocketed to our world from an asteroid storm of planetary crossbreeding.

In other words, our atoms have the same backstory as the rest of the solar system, smashed together in the core of a star as it blew itself to pieces. And these particles have the same backstory as the entire rest of the universe. All of us, and everything in the cosmos, burst out of nothing when the vacuum of space itself suddenly fell apart.

It seemed that life on Earth was the only possibility. Now there are theories in which there could be life across the universe: in roiling far off skies, in oceans of liquid methane, in burning lakes of molten lava, in the chilling void of empty space, and even deep inside stars themselves. There are more planets out there in the universe than there are grains of sand on all the Earth's beaches, deserts, and sand dunes combined. It's pretty hard to imagine that *nowhere* else in the cosmos has even a speck of life. Our galaxy cluster is silently being dragged toward a huge unknown object, and we have no idea why. The entire universe is way larger than the edge of what we can see, and we have no idea how much further it goes.

But none of it will matter in the end because, trillions of years from now, our cosmos will either rip itself to shreds, crush itself into nothing, or expand forever into oblivion, leaving no trace of our existence. Our universe could even recreate itself over again in the distant future. Perhaps all of this has already happened, and you've already read this book. In that case, no refunds.

If none of the previous paragraphs were even slightly unsettling to you, we might have a serious problem.

Since we're in such a stupendously huge universe, we're faced with the sad fact that we'll never be able to grasp it all. The human brain is, after all, only a kilogram of cells in our heads. Most of the universe lies far beyond our reach, either in places too distant to access, too small to observe, too large to comprehend, too far in the past to see, or too far in the future to visualize.

Some people find it chilling, saddening, and somewhat daunting. Others find it thrilling, riveting, exciting, and awe-inspiring. Depending on how you feel about it, this book is either going to be awesome, or a genuine horror story that's based on our *actual* reality. Again, no refunds.

No wonder the scientists during the Age of Enlightenment—an era of philosophical reform in the 1600s and 1700s that included the development of the concept of free speech and thought—had such a hard time getting their point across. For two thousand years following the creation of Aristotle's geocentric model of the universe, people gleefully put Earth at the centre of the entire cosmos. They believed that crystal spheres surrounded the planet, fixing the planets and the stars in their twirling paths around us.

Nobody ever imagined that there was anything wrong with this idea, firstly because it made sense based on what we could see, and secondly because there was a ready-made system at Rome's Campo de' Fiori to burn people at the stake for going against such things. During the Middle Ages, a quick way to end up there was to say that the theories put forth by the Roman Catholic Church were wrong. Giordano Bruno, who theorized that the stars in the sky were actually their own suns with solar systems of planets, was excommunicated and exiled three times, then burned at the stake in 1600 for distributing his heretical views.

Basically, anyone who was foolhardy enough to suggest that our world was *not* the divine centre of the cosmos was pushing their luck, especially given the religious dogma at the time.

While it was known that the planets occasionally looped around in their paths across the sky, the geocentric crystal-sphere model of our universe couldn't explain it, except with a ridiculously complex system of spheres within spheres within spheres that rotated throughout the year. It looked like a gear clock on steroids.

Copernicus saw a simpler, but weird and controversial solution: maybe that looping pattern was just what happened when our Earth went along its orbit around the Sun and passed other planets in *their* looping orbits. Was it possible that the Earth *wasn't* the divine centre of everything?

For his own sake, Copernicus kept quiet about his discovery until 1543, the year he died. A few decades later, in 1610, Galileo Galilei had the audacity to publicly spread the idea—and for doing so, he was put under lifetime house arrest by the Roman Inquisition.

But this paradigm entered public consciousness and changed our concept of the universe forever. Perhaps our position as its special centrepiece wasn't the best explanation for reality after all. Copernicus ushered in a brand-new way of thinking about our place in the universe: simplicity is better than human-centrism. The best explanations of the universe were now the simplest and most concise ideas, and science was no longer required to conform to common beliefs; it was dared to defy them. The universe was never so simple ever again.

Even as our sense of cosmic specialness was crushed, we kept assuming we were finally done after each new discovery.

At the turn of the 20th century, the excitement of earlier scientific discoveries had been fading into memory for over a hundred years. The physicist Lord Kelvin is quoted saying in 1900, for example, "There is nothing new to be discovered in physics now. All that remains is more and more precise measurement."

Of course, as we now know, we hadn't quite discovered everything just yet. Despite being a famed physicist for his work in the field of *thermodynamics*, Kelvin couldn't have imagined the discoveries that were going to be made in the next century as scientists began searching for the constants of our universe. Electrons were discovered; special relativity was formulated; the speed of light became a constant; space and time became relative; the atomic nucleus was found; our galaxy was mapped for the first time and turned out to be over a million times larger than previously thought; other galaxies were discovered beyond our own; the universe was found to be expanding; and the Big Bang theory was first proposed.

And all this was only discovered in the first three decades of the 1900s. At this point, the universe is the ultimate antidote to the human ego.

For most of the day, we aren't thinking about our place in the universe. You probably don't think about the fact that you're standing at a dramatic angle on a curved portion of a massive sphere. You don't enter a town and declare that the houses and buildings are protruding from the side of the Earth, even if you happen to live at the equator. No police officer would give you a speeding ticket because you were rotating around the Earth's axis at a thousand kilometres per hour. It sounds ridiculous to say, "I'd like to meet you after the Earth rotates us into its umbral shadow and obscures the Sun." Of course, we find it easier to say "I'd like to meet you after sunset."

When someone asks you, "What's up?" you are expected to say something like, "Not much, you?" People tend to give you a weird look if you say something like, "The direction opposite the centre of the Earth, as defined by human society."

Our bodies never needed the ability to see where we are in the bigger picture. We evolved two eyes so we could see depth and perspective—an effect known as binocular disparity. That works great when you're trying to run from creatures that are trying to eat you. It also works great when you're trying to run after food you *want* to eat. But at larger distances, perspective disappears. Studies have found that we can't really see perspective in anything farther than twenty metres away.

Unfortunately, the universe is slightly further than twenty metres away.

The cosmos offers a perspective that literally flips our world upside down. Humanity is only a very small part of an enormous story that goes billions of years into the past, trillions of years into the future, deep into the subatomic realm, and out to the furthest galaxies.

Most of our universe is inaccessible, but through observation and inquiry, a little speculation, and the power of scientific imagination, we can make it there. In fact, we can go absolutely anywhere.

Just wait for a day when you can see both the Moon and the Sun in the daytime sky, tilt your head so that both of them are lying in a flat line, and you've just oriented yourself with the rest of the solar system. You're standing on the curved surface of a giant sphere, at an awkward angle, whether you like it or not!

With that said, welcome to the universe.

PART 2

OUR VAST UNIVERSE

THE UNIMAGINABLE IMMENSITY OF SPACE

Let's state the obvious: space is huge. The size of the universe defies our imagination. It reduces our giant planet down to something far less than a speck of dust. There are eight billion people on Earth, but our planet is just one of ten million million billion other planets in the universe.

It's basically useless to try to comprehend the scale of the cosmos just by reading about big numbers on a sheet of paper. To be honest, that is exactly what we're about to do, but hopefully you see the point. Despite the fact that our brains only evolved to think about things within a few metres of us, we might as well try to comprehend the size of the universe anyway.

Only a few spacecraft are currently able to support humans in space, so the human race is still almost completely stuck on the surface. With a diameter of 12,700 kilometres, our world is so gigantic that it takes a wave of sound a whole day and eight hours to circle the equator. At a brisk walking pace, without stopping or sleeping, it would take a little over a year to trek around the Earth.

OUR LOCAL PLANET FAMILY

Our natural satellite, the Moon, is our nearest neighbour. But it's 380,000 kilometres away, which is thirty times the width of our entire planet. While it may look massive in the night sky hanging over the horizon, there's enough space between us and the Moon to fit every other planet in the solar system combined. At the moment, the spacecraft travel time to the Moon is about three days.

This is just a mere footstep into our cosmic backyard. The Moon is 160 times closer than the next nearest world, which is usually Venus or Mars, depending on their orbits. Both of them can get within around 60 million kilometres of Earth. As we prepare for human missions across the inner solar system in the coming decades, we'll need to be prepared to cross a distance 4,800 times wider than our small planet.

The Earth cruises in its orbit around the Sun at a brisk speed of around 30 kilometres per second. Yeah, you're travelling the width of the entire planet every seven minutes. This place, the place in which you're now sitting, was in space when you started reading the last sentence.

The distance between the Earth and the Sun, first accurately measured in 1672 by Giovanni Cassini, is an enormous void: 150 million kilometres. If our planet were the size of a blueberry, the distance from the Earth to the Sun would be the length of a football field. But who cares about snazzy comparisons? We've barely left the inner solar system. Let's keep going.

❖ THE OUTER PLANETS

Space art is cool, but it fails miserably in showing the vast distances between objects in space. The asteroid belt is pictured in artists' renditions as a dense highway of speeding rocks, flying boulders, and awesome collisions, but the real asteroid belt is far less epic.

The typical distance between individual asteroids is about a million kilometres, or 80 times the width of our planet. The asteroids themselves, being only a few kilometres across, would be imperceptible if you looked around you, even in the thickest part of the asteroid belt. Even though the whole belt weighs a quarter of a sextillion tons, that's only three percent of the mass of our Moon, spread out like butter on toast across the entire inner solar system.

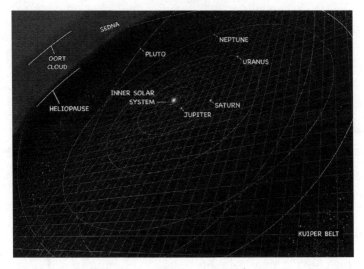

If you took a grain of salt, crushed it up, and sprinkled it across the area of Switzerland, you'd get a sense of how empty our solar system is.

Neptune is often regarded as the edge of the conventional solar system, simply because it encapsulates the asteroid belt and the seven other planets. It traces an enormous orbit around the Sun, around 30 times further away than we are. But our solar system is not finished yet.

Way out in the solar system's deep end, there's a cold and icy field of asteroids, comets, and dwarf planets known as the *Kuiper Belt*, which extends from 30 to 50 times the distance from the Earth to the Sun. While the massive gas giants of Jupiter, Saturn, Uranus, and Neptune basically swept out all the tiny rocks from the solar system with their huge gravitational pull, they couldn't clear out the trillions of rocks in the far outer solar system. This sparse field of cold rocks has some dramatic sights: a distant dwarf planet named Haumea was discovered to have a thin ring around it, which is pretty uncommon for rocky worlds.

❖ THE FURTHEST LIMITS

At around 120 times the distance from the Earth to the Sun, we finally get to the official border between the solar system and interstellar space. Our star produces a powerful barrage of charged particles known as the *solar wind*. As it sweeps past the Earth, the planet's magnetic field channels the particles down into the atmosphere where they generate spectacular aurorae.

The rest of the particles fly straight out to the edge of the solar system. They have so much energy that they billow into a tenuous bubble, or boundary, around the entire solar system, known as the *heliopause*. It marks the conventional edge of the solar system; the Sun's ionizing radiation does not persist beyond that point.

While our star's particle wind can only push 18 billion kilometres into space, the gravity of the Sun easily reaches for trillions of kilometres more, keeping billions of small rocks in massive orbits. This means that the true edge of the solar system isn't for quite a distance longer. Sedna, a distant minor planet, reaches the furthest edge of its orbit at a staggering 940 times the distance from the Earth to the Sun. No one knows much about Sedna, but it takes over eleven thousand years to complete one loop of its orbit; it's around half as wide as Pluto, and its temperature is a chilling –260°C in the summertime.

Beyond even this, we eventually enter a sparse cloud of comets and frozen rocks that are still barely clinging to our Sun's weak gravity. This region is known as the *Oort Cloud*, a theoretical area of the solar system first proposed by Jan Oort in 1950.

Space is nearly a perfect vacuum. And even though it is swarming with quadrillions of pebbles and boulders, they are spaced apart by hundreds of millions of kilo-metres—almost as far away from one another as the diameter of the entire inner solar system.

This cold field of aloof comets could extend as far as 50,000 times the distance from the Earth to the Sun. Only then have we finally reached the edge of our entire solar system. Now it's time to look at the 200 billion other solar systems scattered across our galaxy.

THE MILKY WAY GALAXY

The Sun and its planets are in constant motion throughout the Milky Way as they cruise around the galactic centre in a massive 250-million-year-long orbit. Our own planet is being hurled along at 200 kilometres each second as it makes its long looping journey around the galaxy. The last time our planet was at this exact location in its galactic orbit, the climate was unrecognizable, choked by carbon dioxide in the midst of the *Permian-Triassic Mass Extinction Event*—the most devastating climate disaster the Earth has ever seen. A lot has changed since we were last exactly here.

❖ THE SLOWNESS OF LIGHT

The speed of light is the fastest speed in the universe. Since you started reading this chapter, all the light you emitted has travelled past Mars. Every single second, light travels an impressive 300,000 kilometres.

If you attained the awesome velocity of light, you could circle the entire equator of the Earth in one-seventh of a second. You'd be able to cross the distance from the Earth to the Sun in just eight minutes, and the orbits of the outermost planets would be only a five-hour flight away. At the speed of light, you could leave the solar system in less time than it takes an airliner to fly across the Pacific Ocean. That's blindingly fast. But the galaxy is stupendously huge, and easily beats light's high velocity.

For example, the nearest solar system to ours is a red dwarf star called *Proxima Centauri*, complete with three planets orbiting around it, located 38 trillion kilometres away—that's 8,600 times the distance from our Sun to Neptune. If you booked a trip there and chose light as your premium airline, you'd be flying for over four years.

The voids of space between stars are so bafflingly huge that it's pointless to measure them in miles or kilometres. Light, the fastest traveller in the universe, is actually a pretty convenient way to measure vast distances. Light can travel almost ten trillion kilometres in a year, so we call that distance a light-year.

Most of the stars in our night sky are hundreds, or sometimes thousands of light-years away, and since it takes centuries or even millennia for light to cross that distance, it creates a trippy optical illusion: we're viewing the night sky in the distant past.

❖ A WINDOW INTO THE PAST

The speed of light isn't just the speed limit of photons, but also the speed limit of any object. It is the speed limit of all forces, and indeed the speed limit of any means of communication. It's completely impossible to exceed the speed of light, because any beam of light you shine, any gravitational pull you create, or any magnetic field you generate will reach its maximum velocity only at the speed of light.

If our Sun suddenly disappeared, it would take eight minutes for the darkness to spread to Earth because it takes that long for light to cross that distance; it would also take eight minutes for the sudden loss of gravity to reach us. For eight uncanny minutes, the Earth would still orbit the place where the Sun used to exist.

Light from Proxima Centauri takes four years to reach us, so what we see is four years in the past. If you travelled there in 2024 and peered back at Earth, you'd be witnessing the Covid-19 pandemic just beginning to ravage our society.

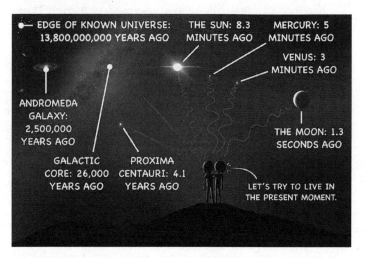

The red supergiant star Betelgeuse, the shoulder of the constellation Orion, is 642 light-years away, and it's about to explode as it approaches the violent end of its lifespan. At any moment, the star will collapse and destroy itself in a brilliant supernova explosion. But for all we know, it might have already exploded. We won't know until we see it, of course, but the blazing glow of light could be on its way to Earth at this very moment— or 600 years from now, or anywhere in between.

Our Milky Way galaxy is around 100,000 light-years across, which is 25,000 times larger than the distance between the Sun and Proxima Centauri. The Sun is located around halfway between the galactic centre and the outer edge, and it's just one of 200 billion stars, most of which have their own families of planets. It takes millennia for light to cross even a small part of our galaxy, and that leads to something really unsettling: most of the galaxy has no idea we exist.

❖ OUR TINY BUBBLE

In the game of life on this planet, we're the newbies. We began forming civilizations around twelve thousand years ago, starting with the early societies of Natufian huts on the western banks of the Jordan River. While our civilization has existed for thousands of years, we really only began tampering with the Earth on a massive level in the 1800s with the industrial revolution.

Primitive wireless radio began in 1906. We only intentionally began beaming radio signals into space in 1974 with the historical Arecibo message. In that message, we sent a coded image that included the human figure, the position of the Earth, and an image of our DNA—including the five elements that compose its double-helix spiral: hydrogen, carbon, nitrogen, oxygen, and phosphorous. It was beamed to M13, a cluster of stars located 25,000 light-years away. If anyone's listening, they won't receive our DM for twenty-five millennia. Even as we blast our Spotify playlists, radio signals and FaceTime calls into the cosmos at full volume, those signals are limited by the speed of light.

Currently, these radio signals have drifted only 50 light-years into the galaxy in all directions. Any extraterrestrial civilization beyond that distance has no idea we ever sent a message, ever. Not a single world beyond 100 light-years has ever heard the BBC, the Saturday Night Live show, or any message humanity has ever accidentally or purposefully leaked into space. The hundred-light-years of range limits the number of potential eavesdroppers to several hundred worlds, which is not a lot given that there could be trillions of worlds in our galaxy alone.

And yet, our civilization itself, by now about 12,000 years old, has produced a sphere of influence spanning over 12,000 light-years. In other words, any planet within 12,000 light-years of us, with powerful enough equipment, could spot us.

But the galaxy is huge, and there's a lot of our galaxy beyond 12,000 light-years. Given the enormity of the Milky Way, which spans 100,000 light-years in width and 8,000 light-years in thickness, our existence has only been revealed to around 1.5% of the entire galaxy. Our civilization's entire 12,000-year-long history is totally invisible to over 98% of the galaxy. From the perspective of most of the Milky Way, we literally don't exist yet. That information is still coming to them.

Any embarrassing thing you do today won't become known to the rest of the galaxy for a hundred millennia. Whether that adds comfort or tension, I do not know.

ALL THE LIGHT EMITTED IN THE LAST 2,000 YEARS.

ALL THE LIGHT EMITTED BY ALL OF HUMAN CIVILIZATION, EVER.

THE REST OF THE GALAXY, BLISSFULLY UNAWARE OF OUR EXISTENCE

❖ LIGHT IMMORTALITY

Apart from making us invisible to the rest of the universe, the speed of light offers a pretty nifty bonus: it lets you live forever. If you're ever worried about the shortness of human life, take a moment to think about all the particles of light you emitted and reflected. You don't need to think about it, because you've been shining light into the universe since the day you were born. All those waves of light are still out there. They're expanding into space at this very moment, drifting away from Earth at 300,000 kilometres per second.

If you live to 90, you'll create a 90-light-year-thick sphere of light that will expand outward into space *forever*. Your image will be a bubble of light and radiation that will drift into space for an infinite amount of time!

If someone in the distant future is in the right location at the right time, and they happen to have a good enough telescope, they'll be able to see you, how you lived your life, the connections you made, and the impact you left, all played out again for this future observer and place.

INTERGALACTIC SPACE

Our galaxy is shaped like an enormous spiral of stars, and while the bulk of its matter is packed inside that spiral, the entire cluster of stars is at least twice as large. A few million lost solar systems are scattered in deep space beyond the main spiral. But our galaxy is actually way larger than this—we just can't see it.

Almost every galaxy in the universe has a cloud of *dark matter* around it. Dark matter is totally invisible; it doesn't emit or absorb light, and it seems to pass right through normal matter. The only reason we know about it is because of gravity, and because galaxies seem to be spinning a whole lot faster than they should be.

You'd expect galaxies to spin like whirlpools, with the central stars whirling around the fastest, and the outer spiral arms slowly trailing behind. But when Vera Rubin observed the spinning galaxies in 1978, she found that the outer edges of galaxies spin at the same rate, more like a rigid pinwheel than a whirlpool.

Essentially, the outer edges of galaxies were spinning too fast; the clouds of stars shouldn't have had enough gravity to keep themselves from being flung off into space. This hinted at the presence of an invisible cloud of some unknown massive stuff holding every galaxy in the universe together, including ours.

Our galaxy's dark matter cloud is a whopping two million light-years across, over twenty times larger than the little star-speckled spiral that we usually think of as the *entire* Milky Way. In fact, dark matter is so densely clouded that it outweighs all the regular matter in the universe by over five times.

At a distance of 2.5 million light-years, or around 25 times the width of our galaxy, we finally get to our closest galactic neighbour, the *Andromeda Galaxy*, consisting of about one trillion stars. For every star we have in our galaxy, it's got five. Just think of the quadrillions of planets that must exist within it. The Andromeda galaxy, however, is currently being seen as it appeared 2.5 million years in the past. We'll never know what has happened there in the time since then. Whole civilizations could have risen and fallen before any hint of their existence reaches us. Any message we send to them would be like mailing a postcard on a snail—literal snail mail. It takes so remarkably long for light to travel from the Milky Way to Andromeda that from *their* point of view, the Earth currently appears to be in the Pleistocene Era, right in the middle of a massive global ice age. *Homo sapiens*, the modern human species, didn't even exist back then. What a difference a few million years makes.

❖ OUR GALACTIC NEIGHBOURS

Together, the Milky Way and the Andromeda Galaxy are two members of a massive encompassing cluster of around 150 galaxies known as the *Local Group*, if it even makes sense to consider tens of millions of light-years to be "local" at all—of course, the word "local" is used rather liberally in astronomy.

As our universe expands, most galaxies will drift away from each other, but our Local Group will remain bonded together by gravity; these galaxies are going to be with us for the long haul. In fact, the Local Group is so intimate that in around one trillion years, most of the 150 known galaxies in the group will merge together to form one galaxy to rule them all.

Our galaxy is destined to meet a similar fate, but sooner. In 1959, two astronomers named Franz Kahn and Lodewijk Woltjer looked at how the Milky Way was dancing around our galactic neighbour of Andromeda. They predicted that in around five billion years, the two galaxies would splash and crash in a dazzling display of galactic pinball, merging together to form a single galaxy.

Contrary to popular belief, there wouldn't be much mortal peril living on a planet in a colliding galaxy; there's simply too much space within galaxies for star collisions to be a concern. While galaxies appear to be bulky objects shrouded in thick gas and dust, they're actually almost completely empty, and usually just flow through each other. Even with two galaxies crashing straight through each other, the odds of solar systems smashing together are nearly zero.

Our Local Group of galaxies is one of several clusters of galaxies in the cosmic vicinity. All of our neighbouring galaxy clusters are each held together by gravity, but they're completely separate from one another.

The nearest galaxy cluster is the *Maffei Group*, already separated from us by ten million light-years, a distance 100 times wider than our entire galaxy. For some reason, the Maffei Group is rocketing away from us extremely fast—much faster than it ought to be, given that our universe is expanding fairly slowly. A 1993 study suspected that the Maffei Group may have been blasted away from our own Local Group following some cataclysmic galactic pinball several billion years ago. Galactic pinball seems to be a timeless sport.

❖ THE GALACTIC SUPERCLUSTER

Together, the Local Group, the Maffei Group, and about 100 other galaxy groups compose a mind-numbingly vast chain of galaxy clusters known as the *Laniakea Supercluster*, which spans an awesome 520 million light-years and contains about a quintillion individual stars.

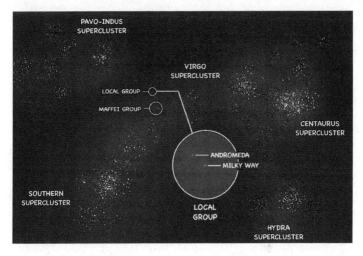

The size difference between the Earth and the Laniakea supercluster is about the same as the size difference between an atom and the Earth. If you look back to the introduction, it was mentioned that the Earth is just a speck of dust. That was a lie; we're even less than that.

The galaxies of our supercluster are in constant motion through space, and while you'd expect this motion to be random, observations in the 1970s found that our galaxy and several hundred thousand others are quietly being dragged toward an unknown gravity source, known as the *Great Attractor*, which is estimated to weigh as much as fifty quadrillion suns.

What could create such a behemoth gravitational pull—strong enough to lure a hundred thousand galaxies at speeds of around 600 kilometres per second?

Our universe is constantly shifting, and while the distant parts of the cosmos expand away from us, nearby galaxy clusters naturally pull themselves together, flowing toward the densest region of space. The entire Laniakea Supercluster, for example, is gradually flowing toward a super-dense region of the *Norma Cluster*.

The Great Attractor isn't a monstrous singular object, but an enormous region of space packed with thousands of galaxies. Our galactic supercluster, on the largest scales, behaves a lot like a liquid—a sloshing ocean of quintillions of stars in millions of galaxies. We, on our speck of dust, are simply following the tide.

❖ COSMIC THRILL RIDE

Our little planet, rotating around its axis, orbiting around the Sun, cruising around the Milky Way, and drifting through intergalactic space, is being rocketed along at over two million kilometres per hour.

People tend to enjoy visiting the place where they were born, the place where they fell in love, places where childhood memories were made, or seeing plaques that mark the locations of important events. But our planet is careening through the cosmos at such insane speeds that it's absolutely impossible to revisit those places. Since you began reading this paragraph, you've travelled twice the width of our entire planet through space. At the time of writing, World War II happened in a place in space that is now over three hundred times further away than the edge of our solar system. Three days ago, you were about as far away from here as the Sun.

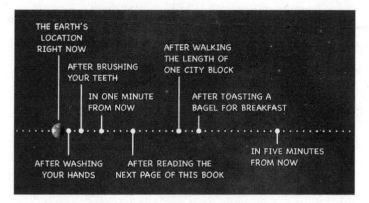

THE EARTH'S
LOCATION
RIGHT NOW

AFTER WALKING
THE LENGTH OF
ONE CITY BLOCK

AFTER BRUSHING
YOUR TEETH

IN ONE MINUTE
FROM NOW

AFTER TOASTING A
BAGEL FOR BREAKFAST

AFTER WASHING
YOUR HANDS

AFTER READING THE
NEXT PAGE OF THIS BOOK

IN FIVE MINUTES
FROM NOW

It's okay. Take a moment to sit still.

The Laniakea Supercluster is enormous, but it's only one of about ten million superclusters across the observable universe, and its staggering size only represents 0.000015% of the total volume of our cosmos.

At the largest scales of our universe, superclusters join together to form spindles, filaments and bubbles of absurd sizes. Billions of galaxies form a dazzling structure known as the *cosmic web*, with long bridges of superclusters linking together around giant voids of pure nothingness.

❖ THE TERRORS OF THE COSMOS

We live in a peaceful region of space free from terrifying menaces that roam the universe. Out there in the depths of the cosmos, there are places that put even the most ludicrous sci-fi weapons to shame.

TON 618, one of the largest black holes known, is 60 billion times more massive than the Sun. It literally weighs as much as an entire galaxy, and the hole itself is 30 times wider than our entire solar system.

When Marie-Helene Ulrich discovered it back in 1976, nobody imagined it was over 18 billion light-years away: it was bright enough to spot with a small telescope on a clear night. It shines with the incredible brilliance of 140 trillion suns—almost a thousand times brighter than our entire galaxy. The black hole itself is completely dark; no light can escape. The light we see comes from the gas, dust, planets and stars that are unlucky enough to fall in; they're ripped into subatomic particles, heated to around 10 million degrees Celsius, and accelerated to almost the speed of light. It's nothing short of the worst massage ever.

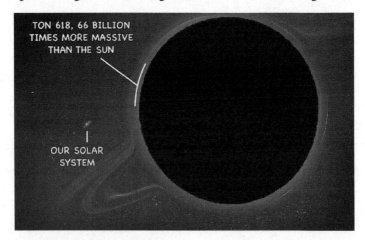

TON 618, 66 BILLION TIMES MORE MASSIVE THAN THE SUN

OUR SOLAR SYSTEM

Much closer to home, a supermassive black hole punched a chasm into the Ophiuchus Cluster of galaxies, 390 million light-years away. It erupted with a total energy of a billion trillion trillion trillion tons of TNT, which is like an entire galaxy's worth of stars going supernova at the same time.

The fallout from the explosion blasted a whole super-cluster of galaxies apart, forming a void around fifteen times wider than our entire galaxy. If we had been in the explosion's line of fire, our entire solar system would have been dissolved into subatomic plasma in an instant. Like a drop of water sizzling on a frying pan, our planet would have just evaporated.

When we stare at the other stars in our galaxy, we're looking a few hundred years into the past. But when we look at galaxies across the universe, we're looking billions of years into the past. The galaxies back then didn't look much like they do today. The universe was still a chaotic maelstrom of colliding galaxies, exploding stars, and the real monsters of the cosmos: quasars.

Quasi-stellar radio sources, more easily known as *quasars*, were huge black holes on steroids, located at the centres of galaxies which they consumed slowly. They were bright enough to outshine their entire galaxy clusters, consuming stars at a ferocious rate of about one Sun per day and blasting their remains into space as a hot plasma, moving outward at nearly the speed of light. The beams themselves, like a cosmic Death Star, punched millions of light-years into the void of space, easily stretching a dozen times the width of our entire galaxy. Anything in the vicinity of a quasar was doused with gamma radiation, which would have sterilized every planet caught in its gaze.

By now, the era of quasars has come to an end, their remnants have quieted down, and they've eaten through all their fuel. Was life possible during the age of quasars? It inevitably makes us wonder if this is why we exist *now* in the universe's timeline instead of *then*.

Indeed, there are places out there that are best left unvisited.

EVERYTHING WE CAN SEE

As we zoom out of our supercluster, our little galaxy quickly diminishes into a speck of dust, easily lost in an endless ocean of two trillion (2,000,000,000,000) galaxies and a septillion (1,000,000,000,000,000,00 0,000,000) stars speckling our cosmos. All evidence suggests that most of the stars in the universe have planets around them. If there's over a septillion planets out there in the cosmos, that's more planets than all the grains of sand on every beach and desert on Earth combined.

A fun trick to picture the absurd scale of the universe is, oddly enough, to cover it up. On a clear night, head outside and look up at the stars. Now, raise your hand and stick out your thumb, holding it up against the sky. If you're standing in a dark place, you might be able to see several stars behind your thumb; if you're standing in the middle of a city, you might see nothing at all. But it doesn't matter; everything's still there, even if you can't see it. Right behind your thumb, hidden from your view, are about 200 billion galaxies. Those galaxies might contain some 10 sextillion planets, all under your thumb.

❖ THE EDGE OF WHAT WE CAN SEE

The further away an object is from us, the longer it takes light to cross the distance. For a galaxy that is 10 billion light-years away, it would take 10 billion years for light to reach us, so we would only be able to see that galaxy as it appeared 10 billion years in the past.

Our universe was most likely born in a fiery explosion, the Big Bang, a mere 13.8 billion years in the past. That means there hasn't been enough time—in the entire history of the universe—for light from further than 13.8 billion light-years to reach us. Galaxies definitely exist in places further away than that, but any light from those distant objects is still on its journey to us.

Our universe is also expanding, so the distances between objects are increasing. Like an inflating balloon, the light travelling between objects gets spaced out and stretched, lengthening its waves, giving the distant galaxies a dim reddish hue. The galaxies themselves aren't red, but their light has been stretched so much by the universe's expansion—a process known as *redshift*—that they now appear a deep crimson. After taking into account the expansion of our universe, the most distant objects we can see are around 46.5 billion light-years away.

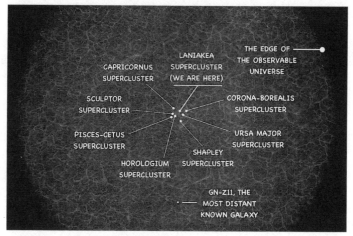

Since we can only see up to the same 46.5-billion-light-year limit in all directions, we see ourselves as the centre of a massive sphere that's 46.5 billion light-years in radius, encapsulating a huge bubble of galaxies 93 billion light-years wide. This sphere is known as the *observable universe*: everything we can possibly see. Nothing that happens beyond the edge—no smashing galaxies, no exploding stars, no alien civilization, no *Star Wars* space battles, and no radio message sent—will *ever* reach us. Ever.

❖ A MATTER OF PERSPECTIVE

When we look at distant galaxies at the very edge of our observable universe, we see them as they appeared in the distant past. From our point of view, they're almost 13.8 billion light-years away, so we're seeing them as they looked right after they came out of the oven—quite literally, given that the Big Bang had just happened.

Some of them look like messy splotches of unkempt stars, likely with no planets or primordial solar systems. From their perspective, however, it's *we* who are on the edge of *their* observable universe. They would see a version of our Milky Way galaxy that we can't even imagine: they'd see a distant relic of the past in which our solar system hadn't even formed yet.

They wouldn't know that at this very moment, that old and shabby galaxy now contains an intelligent form of life, 13.8 billion years later: ourselves.

Similarly to their conundrum, we're looking at these galaxies as they appeared almost fourteen billion years ago. They could be home to exotic galaxy-spanning civilizations by now, but we can only see them in their infancy.

No matter where we are in the universe, we will always see ourselves as being the centre of our own observable universe, because all light has to travel an equal distance to reach us from the edge. In a very annoying way, the distant galaxies in *our* observable universe can see an entire portion of *their* observable universe that is completely invisible to us, beyond our cosmic horizon but not theirs.

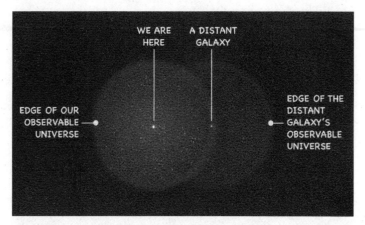

There are quadrillions of planets, maybe with trillions of alien life forms, which we will never be able to contact. Our vision is limited to a small window of an enormous universe, the full extent of which is still a mystery. We're locked away in a little bubble in a vast ocean, and under the known laws of physics, it doesn't look like we're getting out anytime soon!

❖ THE ESCAPING GALAXIES

Our observable universe is 93 billion light-years across, but its amazing size is an illusion. The universe is expanding quickly, and that limits the amount of the universe we can access.

Nearby galaxies are expanding away from us at hundreds of kilometres per second, but distant galaxies are slipping away at hundreds of thousands of kilometres per second—near the speed of light. Beyond a certain distance, in fact, galaxies are pushed away from us *faster* than the speed of light, making them invisible, and totally impossible to reach.

That critical distance—the point at which objects are pushed away faster than light—is around fourteen billion light-years. Any galaxy beyond that distance is never going to be seen again; they're basically gone from the observable universe itself. The only reason we can still see those distant galaxies in our sky is because it has taken so absurdly long for their light to reach us. The light of ancient, long-gone galaxies is just finally reaching us today, which is somewhat haunting. The galaxies themselves have disappeared over the edge a long time ago, but their images remain.

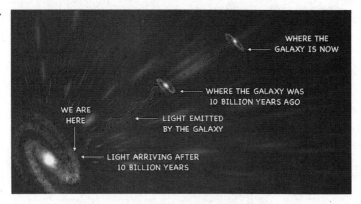

A devastating 94% of all the galaxies in our skies are already gone from the observable universe; they've already slipped past our cosmic horizon. In the time it took you to read that last sentence, about ten million planets slipped over the edge and are now gone from us forever, never to be seen again. If there were distant civilizations on any of them, we'll never know.

BEYOND THE OBSERVABLE UNIVERSE

It is normal to feel utterly small when thinking about the fact that our entire observable universe is likely not the *entire* universe.

Since the beginning of human history, our species has wondered whether the universe goes for a large but finite distance out into space, or whether it literally goes on *forever*. Does our cosmos stretch endlessly into the void, or would we eventually hit a border and come to an edge? Neither option sounds comforting at face value, and when you look into the details, they both sound downright *terrifying*.

❖ A FINITE UNIVERSE

If the universe were finite, we might expect to find some cosmic border somewhere extremely far from here. Perhaps a dividing wall, built into space itself, marks the edge of our universe. A finite cosmos seemingly requires a hard edge—a point at which space suddenly ends. If this sounds oddly similar to the flat-earth conspiracy, it should seem obvious how wrong this model of the universe is.

If our universe had a border, it would also have a centre point. We have no clue where the centre of the universe is, and all evidence suggests there is none. If there were, gravity would have slowly pulled the universe toward the middle, like a bunch of balls on a trampoline rolling toward the centre.

Given that space appears the same everywhere in the cosmos, it would be extremely weird to have a sudden point where it all ended. And then what? If you've put a border around the universe, what's beyond the border? If it's just more space, then what causes all the galaxies to stay in the space inside the border? If it's not space, then what could it possibly be?

The concept of a finite universe has dozens of problems that go against the theories we currently believe are true, so most cosmologists just accept the No-Boundary Principle, which is a fancy way of saying that our universe has no edge.

In tackling the strange mystery of whether the universe is infinite or finite, the first decent attempt was made by the Roman philosopher Titus Lucretius Carus. He proposed the *Javelin Argument*, a thought experiment that begins with a person standing on a mountain with a javelin.

If you throw a javelin as far as you can, that javelin might fly onward forever, proving that the universe is infinite. But it also might hit a distant mountain and fall to the ground, where you could pick it up, climb to the peak of *that* mountain, and throw it again. The universe must be infinite, he argued, because beyond each mountain, there'd simply be another vast landscape.

While this was a decent first attempt, it was just a thought experiment. Now, two thousand years later, we have real scientific evidence in cosmology and astrophysics to back us up.

❖ SPHERICAL SPACE

When Einstein formulated his theory of general relativity in 1915, he completely crushed the notion that space was rigid and unchanging, revealing that our universe was a dynamic thing that could bend with mass, stretch with gravity, and even ripple along with twirling orbits. The Earth is massive enough to have warped space into a gravitational dimple, holding all eight billion of us captive within its walls, and keeping the Moon in a spiralling orbit like a coin rolling around a funnel.

The discovery of space's curviness allowed us, for the first time, to grapple with the true size and shape of the entire—not just the observable—universe.

Einstein realized that our universe could have no edge or border, and *still* be finite in size. He imagined that if gravity were strong enough throughout the universe, it could pull and drag on space itself, causing the universe to curve in upon itself, curling it into a sphere.

A sphere has no edges but is still finite in size. You can walk forever in a straight line on the surface of the Earth, but that doesn't mean our planet is infinite; you just walk in a circle around the world and arrive back where you began. In this sense, our entire universe might be a three-dimensional surface wrapped into a *four-dimensional* sphere. The fourth dimension is something we cannot even begin to imagine. Our 3D brains just aren't built for it, and no amount of coffee will possibly help you grasp it. Picture it as a direction that extends perpendicular to all the directions of 3D space. It isn't up, down, left, right, forward, or backward—it extends outward. It exists outside our reality altogether. In this model of the universe, every planet and star in the cosmos, Earth included, may be three-dimensional objects existing on the curved surface of a hypersphere.

How's *that* for adding some new dimensions to your life?

❖ SEARCHING FOR THE CURVES

The size of our entire cosmos is literally a matter of gravity. If the force of gravity grips our universe stronger, it will curve space more dramatically, curling it into a small, tightly packed sphere. On the other hand, a more gentle pull from gravity could allow our universe to bend more subtly, forming a shallow curve and an extremely large sphere.

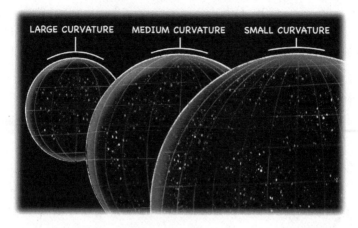

To determine how big the cosmos truly is, all we need to do is measure the curvature. We don't even need to see the whole universe; we just need to see enough of it to see the curvature. For example, you can't see the entire Earth from the vantage point of an airplane, but you can see enough of the curvature to calculate how large the whole planet is. In the same way, even with only a tiny fraction of the universe visible to us, we can figure out the size of the whole thing.

The Wilkinson Microwave Anisotropy Probe, known as the *WMAP satellite*, studied this exact problem for nearly a decade following its launch in 2001.

To say that it's difficult to measure the four-dimensional curvature of our universe would be an understatement. We and our scientific instruments are a part of space, so when space itself is curved, we're curved right along with it. For that reason, our view of the cosmos is deceptive; no matter how warped the universe is, we will always see a "normal" view, making it absurdly difficult to detect that curvature.

However, the WMAP satellite used a more cunning approach: it looked at how light itself was distorted. On the surface of a sphere, light no longer travels in straight lines, but rather moves in curves along a circular path. The curving of the light makes distant objects look larger than they really are, adding a weird distortion to what we see when we peer into space. The WMAP satellite looked at the oldest, most distant light in the universe, which had travelled nearly 14 billion light-years through space. If there were any curvature, surely that light would show it.

Despite nearly a decade of searching, the results from the WMAP mission, published in 2013, were initially disappointing: our universe's curvature was found to be almost exactly zero, with just a 0.4% margin of error.

I say "*initially* disappointing" because the implications of having almost *no* curvature are even more absurd than having a *lot* of curvature. If the WMAP mission had found an obvious curvature, it would have implied that our cosmos was a fairly small sphere—maybe only a couple hundred billion light-years all around. But if our cosmos is so large that the curvature isn't even visible across our *entire* observable universe, then the cosmos is incredibly large.

❖ A LARGER UNIVERSE

When the WMAP results were released, astronomers calculated that the bare minimum possible size of the entire cosmos is approximately 250 times larger than our little observable universe, and that's a conservative estimate; it could be as much as 400.

The closer our universe is to zero curvature, the larger it is. Unless our universe's curvature is *exactly* zero, we can't really know how large the universe is because its curvature might be too shallow for our instruments to detect. We might accidentally conclude that our universe has exactly zero curvature, even if it *was* curved just a little. It's like how you might accidentally conclude the Earth had zero curvature if you were just looking at the horizon from the ground. Like flat-Earthers do.

The physicist Alan Guth proposed that when our universe initially exploded in the Big Bang and blew up in cosmic inflation—an event we'll dive into later in this book—it might have expanded faster than the speed of light. He predicted that, at that absurd rate of expansion, our current universe should be around 1.4 *decillion* light-years across, which is around fourteen million million million million million million million million million million million times more spacious than our tiny observable universe!

Just imagine what marvels could exist in a universe this mind-meltingly huge. If it's really that large, our cosmos should contain over 10^{79} galaxies with about 10^{90} stars and planets. That's around ten billion times more planets than there are *atoms* in our entire observable universe. At this scale, numbers mean nothing, but they make us want to ask one burning question: how can we possibly be alone in the universe?

AN INFINITE UNIVERSE

While our universe may subtly curve itself into a four-dimensional sphere of truly astronomical size, there's an even more baffling possibility: maybe our universe has no curvature at all, causing it to be infinitely large. That's certainly what the WMAP satellite suggested. Since then, results from the Planck satellite have provided additional evidence for a flat universe.

❖ SPACE WITHOUT THE CURVES

But wait! A flat universe, for clarification, isn't really flat. It still has all three dimensions of space, just with no curvature in the fourth dimension. It's like a sheet of paper lying completely flat against the ground. Therefore, while the Flat Earth Society continues to have conflict with the scientific community, the lesser-known Flat *Universe* Society has an entire set of cosmological studies to back its case.

If our universe were flat, it would mean it couldn't possibly have curved inward upon itself to make a sphere, which leaves us with only one possibility: it has to be infinite in size. Space has to extend onward forever, infinitely far in all directions, because it wouldn't make sense to hit a cosmic border at the edge.

If our universe is infinite in size, our observable universe shrinks down to absolutely nothing in the big picture, which is as awesome as it is terrifying. No matter how far our telescopes can gaze, and no matter how far humanity goes, we will have reached exactly zero percent of an infinite universe. No matter how far we go, there will always be an infinite distance ahead.

This might not bother you particularly; you may not have been planning on visiting every destination in the universe anyway. But consider that astronomy, cosmology, physics, chemistry, biology, and all of science are based on the laws and principles we observe and measure to be true within our own observable universe. If that whole observable universe is actually 0% of the whole universe, we don't have much of a sample size to work with.

While we like to assume that the rest of the infinite universe would be the same as the tiny bit of space we live in, we can't definitively prove anything beyond our little cosmic horizon.

❖ HITTING THE JACKPOT

If you want to win the lottery, you should buy as many tickets as possible. If you purchase just a single ticket, your odds of winning might be something like one-in-a-million. But if you somehow purchase a trillion lottery tickets, you will almost certainly win—and you'll probably win multiple times. But if you purchase infinite lottery tickets, you're 100% guaranteed to hit the jackpot infinitely many times.

But before you go and buy infinite tickets, let's talk about some other issues first.

While probability is usually a matter of random chance, we don't need to worry about the odds in an infinite cosmos, because no matter how unlikely it is to occur, it's guaranteed to occur an infinite number of times. Anything times infinity is always infinity.

The implications of this simple truth are beyond terrifying.

If our universe is infinite, it contains an infinite number of galaxies containing an infinite number of stars and an infinite number of planets. A small fraction of those planets will evolve life, but a small fraction of infinity is still infinity. A tiny amount of those basic alien life forms will evolve into intelligent civilizations, but again, this would still be an infinite amount.

If the universe is infinite, we get an obvious answer to the question of whether we're alone in the universe: NO. It's honestly a bit of a letdown, since it would be so much more exciting to discover the answer ourselves rather than getting our answer based on math.

But we can go beyond just alien life. While our own observable universe is a lovely way to arrange a billion trillion trillion trillion trillion trillion trillion atoms, it's certainly not the only way to arrange the universe. Think of an infinite universe like a random number generator. It contains an infinite number of observable universes, all lined up next to each other like giant boxes. Inside each observable universe, there are approximately 10^{80} atoms, and each observable universe has a different arrangement.

Within this huge collection of possibilities, you'd be guaranteed to find every possible event, every planet and galaxy, every parallel world, every alien space battle and galactic empire, and every fictional event we have ever dreamed up. In an infinite cosmos, all of these possible universes are realities. Planets and stars and aliens and spaceship battles are just collections of atoms arranged in specific ways. In an infinite universe, since there's infinite space and infinite atoms, there has to be every possible arrangement of matter and energy. And all those things wouldn't just exist *once*; they'd exist an *infinite* number of times.

That includes us, by the way!

❖ IN THE MIDDLE OF NOWHERE

In 2003, the MIT physicist Max Tegmark calculated the bizarre coincidences you'd find in an infinite universe. Based on his analysis, if you jumped into a spaceship and rocketed through space, travelling about 10^{115} orders of magnitude longer than the width of our entire observable universe, you'd probably find a copy of *this* universe.

That distant region of space would contain two trillion identical galaxies. One of those galaxies would have a perfect copy of our solar system. The third planet in that system would be identical to Earth, harbouring a species that looks and behaves just like we do. If you know where you're currently sitting on Earth, you'd be able to meet the exact copy of you currently reading this exact line.

An infinite universe wouldn't just have an endless supply of copies of Earth; it would also have infinitely many *different* versions of Earth. Absurdly far from here, there are Earths getting killed by a meteor, ripped apart by a black hole, or even conquered by a galactic empire. Every moment we avoid nuclear war, an infinite number of copies of Earth are blown to pieces. Every time we've decided to do anything, there's another copy of Earth, somewhere else in the universe, where we didn't. Infinitely many copies of you are already done reading this book. Once again, no refunds.

We're really living in the middle of nowhere. We think of people as being special, and perhaps that's because they're unique. But no matter how unique you are, you're still just *one* possible way to arrange seven octillion atoms.

You're a unique collection of information, but in a universe where there's infinite information, the specific combo that we call "you" has to show up infinitely many times. If you're not the only "you" in this universe, what does the concept of "you" even mean? Or perhaps our universe is finite and you don't need to worry about any of this.

❖ WE ARE AWESOMELY SMALL

Who knows how colossal the universe is? The solar system may be vast, but in comparison to the cosmos, it's our cozy cosmic home. Maybe there are other copies of you out there, ridiculously far away, but you don't need to worry about them, and they don't need to worry about you. Our observable universe is still awesomely huge, filled with trillions of galaxies, and—it bears repeating—more planets than there are grains of sand on all the Earth's beaches.

While our observable universe may only be a tiny fraction of everything in existence, it's definitely large enough for us.

PART 3

THE ORIGIN STORY

THE GREATEST BACKSTORY OF ALL TIME

Many children ask where babies come from. Too often, the response is the standard love story, the union of an egg and sperm, the passing of certain dominant or recessive traits from the mother and the father, and so on.

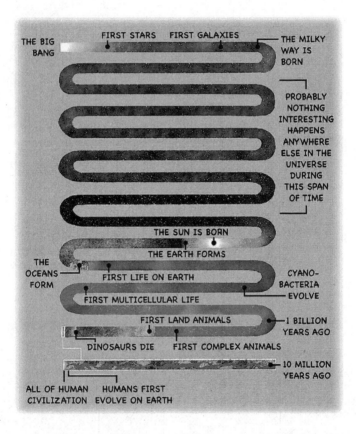

The idea that babies come from a sperm and an egg has always felt rather lacking in plot development. It doesn't have a riveting backstory, and it falls severely short in dramatic effect. *Of course* a baby comes from two parents. But what about the origins of those parents? What about their grandparents? What about the origins of life and the universe? Let's put an end to the boring and typical origin story. Let's go a little bigger than just the parents.

THE MATTER THAT MAKES US

Our bodies are made of cells and atoms, and while it's certainly nice to imagine that these pieces stay locked in place inside our bodies, the truth is rather unsettling. Our bodies are always replacing themselves, behaving less like solid organisms and more like temporary collections of stuff that rapidly evolve and change over time.

Every part of your body is involved in this constant change: the shedding of skin, the eating and excreting of food and water, your cells burning sugar and releasing CO_2 while you inhale and exhale air, and the constant death of old cells and birth of new ones. All this bodily recycling causes our atoms to swap themselves at a feverish rate.

❖ OUR TEMPORARY BODIES

Based on a 1953 study at the Oak Ridge Atomic Research Center in Tennessee, we only keep one in fifty atoms from the previous year, meaning 98% of our bodies wither away into the environment around us annually. About every seven years, the atoms of our bodies are completely recycled—if you're older than seven, you've been alive for some period of time in which you didn't contain a single atom of your present-day body.

Since you started reading this sentence, around ten million of your cells have died and are being replaced. Over the course of your lifespan, you'll end up cycling through around 500 times your own body weight in cells, and your current body is only a tiny temporary part of that huge mass.

This raises tons of existential questions. For example, if your atoms and cells are not even the same as they were seven years ago, what causes your consciousness to continue without being interrupted? How do your experiences survive the swapping and replacing of the atoms in your brain? If you really know the answer, a lot of people would like to speak with you.

If we play back the timeline, you didn't really begin with a fortunate sperm and egg meeting each other. Instead, the evolving chemical reaction that eventually *became* you was *initiated* with the meeting of a sperm and egg. The actual matter that's in your body had already existed a long time before you were born, or even conceived.

A typical breath of fresh air contains around 10^{22} molecules, while the Earth's atmosphere contains around 10^{44} molecules within it. That means, due to a neat coincidence, there are about as many molecules in one breath as there are breaths in the atmosphere. So, if our atmosphere is mixed up well enough, then each breath you take contains about one atom from every breath of every individual in the history of the human species, and indeed the entire history of breathing life itself. The backstory of our atoms is truly breathtaking.

❖ CRASHING PLANETS

In 1974, two planetary scientists, William Hartmann and Donald Davis, proposed that our Moon was created after a spectacular cascade of planetary pinball approximately 4.5 billion years ago. The early solar system was a chaotic place, filled with careening worlds that constantly collided and smashed apart. Our Earth was no exception.

The young Earth orbited the Sun along with about a hundred other planet-sized objects rivalling it. A popular idea is that a planet about the size of Mars, named *Theia* after the titan in Greek mythology, slammed into the Earth and was instantly destroyed, blasting a massive chunk of our planet into space. The debris that settled in the aftermath of the collision was what eventually clumped together under its gravity to form our Moon.

More recently, the situation's been looking even worse for the Earth; a 2018 study proposed that the Earth was actually vaporized in the collision, forming a hot cloud of steamy rock vapour called a *synestia*, which eventually settled back into two separate worlds. Studies have found that around 4/5 of our Moon came from this planetary wrecking ball, which means that about 1/10 of our Earth is composed of Theia remnants.

So, almost an octillion of the atoms in your body were once part of a runaway planet in the early solar system, and as a result, we share a striking amount in common with the Moon. No wonder the Earth and the Moon share almost identical amounts of special oxygen isotopes in their rocks; they were mixed from the same world.

THE ORIGINS OF LIFE

No matter your family history, you are part of an unbroken lineage that goes all the way back across four billion years of history. Somewhere on Earth, a dead collection of molecules became alive and started multiplying, changing the future of our planet forever and, for better or for worse, leading to the evolution of humans.

Okay, that's easy enough to *say*. But *how* did that happen?

Life isn't the easiest thing to brew, even in a chemical mixing lab the size of the Earth's oceans. As a matter of fact, the early environment on Earth wasn't always geared toward life as we know it.

❖ THE LIVELY BEGINNING

Around four billion years ago, the forecast wasn't rain, snow, or clouds—it was rocks. An era of the solar system's history known as the *Late Heavy Bombardment* was happening. Every day, millions of meteors slammed into the Earth, pockmarking it with craters and turning a quarter of its surface into lava.

While this might sound awful, the space hailstorm was a major factor in delivering the raw ingredients for life as we know it. Many of the nutrients in your body likely didn't come from this planet, but from space.

In 1969, a meteorite smashed into the ground just outside the town of Murchison, Australia. That meteorite had huge stores of amino acids and lipids inside it that had been cooked and crusted onto the rock from scalding UV rays in deep space. Could the proteins and fats in our bodies today have been baked in deep space on the surfaces of asteroids that later fell to Earth?

Amino acids—the basic components of proteins—might have actually been cooked up by lightning bolts high in our atmosphere. The famous 1952 Miller-Urey experiment showed that some of the basic ingredients for life could be made with electricity. The experiment produced hot amino acids and sugars by zapping a sample of methane and hydrogen gas. The smoky plumes of early volcanic eruptions were statically charged, and lightning was common. Maybe that's where the stuff of life found its origins.

So, when did all these basic bits and pieces finally come together to make something alive? What are we actually looking for when we ask, "When did life first evolve?" We're not looking for fish, that's for sure, but should we be looking for single cells? Should we lower our standards even more?

To help us, let's take NASA's usual definition of life: any self-sustaining chemical system capable of Darwinian evolution.

That means, by a *very* abstract definition, we finally got "life" on Earth when a little thing could keep itself alive, could reproduce and make copies of itself, and could slowly adapt to its environment over many generations. As soon as that happened, life began.

❖ THE GENETIC CODE

The first step in creating life on Earth was to find a way to carry information. Life has to reproduce, and in order to make offspring, it needs a method to copy and paste its genetic code.

The first thing that comes to mind is DNA.

DNA is shaped like a twisted ladder, and every rung along that ladder—known as a *nucleotide*—is like a letter in a massive book, or a binary digit in a very long string of code. DNA is the program that guides molecules to do something other than bounce around randomly.

It tells cells when to grow, where to do tasks, and how to keep themselves alive. DNA packs an astonishing amount of data into its little strands: every cell in your body, for example, has around three gigabytes of DNA, making your body the best USB hard drive in the world—so far.

Four billion years ago, things were less complicated. Tiny amino acids and nucleotides just floated in the ocean and bounced off each other. Little molecules were coming together and breaking apart all over the place. It was all trial and error. It was like taking a box of Lego bricks, hurling them at a wall, and seeing what came out.

At some point, a basic string of genetic code did come together, but it probably wasn't DNA, and here's why: DNA can't make copies of itself.

In order to reproduce, DNA needs help from special proteins that can read the genetic code and stitch together a new strand. That's fine. But where did the proteins come from? Those proteins are made of tiny amino acids. The amino acids are stitched together in a special pattern that's based on the genetic code in DNA—but if you want to make a strand of DNA, you need proteins, which have to be put together based on a strand of DNA. And… repeat.

It's a chicken-or-egg problem with DNA and proteins. That's why many biologists think that it wasn't DNA that started life on Earth, but rather its more basic single-stranded cousin: a molecule known as RNA, or ribonucleic acid.

A strand of RNA is really just half of a strand of DNA, and even though both of their structures are very similar, RNA has several huge advantages. Firstly, it's simpler. Instead of a double-helix, it only has a single one. With half the complexity, RNA would have appeared in the oceans quicker than DNA.

The more important advantage is this: RNA is a crafty molecule. It can carry a genetic code, but it can *also* work like a protein and copy itself. While DNA needs help from other proteins, RNA can do it all by itself.

In 2018, researchers at the MRC Laboratory of Molecular Biology made a little package of RNA, called a *ribozyme*, that could grab a piece of itself and copy it, making a brand-new package of RNA that could *also* fold up into its own ribozyme.

If a basic piece of RNA came together in the ocean four billion years ago, it might've folded up into one of these ribozymes. If that's what happened, it would make sense why RNA was so successful: it lived solo. It didn't need help from anything else. This idea, in which RNA started life on this planet, is called the *RNA world hypothesis*. RNA is definitely not a simple molecule, but the fact that it can copy and paste *itself* means that it didn't require any fancy coincidences of A and B being in the same place at the same time.

The RNA world hypothesis isn't fully accepted, but if it's true, then every strain of life on this planet—humans included—can trace their origins back to a tiny group of molecules in the middle of the ocean, almost four billion years ago. Great. But how the heck do we go from RNA to modern humans?

❖ A PACKAGE FOR LIFE

It was great to have RNA and proteins floating endlessly around the ocean, but we wouldn't have gone anywhere with that—not unless they were all packaged up in a small cell.

For life to be effective at surviving, it needs to exist in a solid and compact organism. On the long journey from basic RNA to humans, that's Step One.

When you pour oil into water, the droplets of oil don't mix, but rather pool up into little balls that stay separate from the water around them. In the oceans, or perhaps in hot springs filled with boiling water, a similar process might have happened as positive and negative charged liquids, known as polyamines, came together to make tiny bubbles known as *coacervates*.

These bubbles were absolutely tiny—about a dozen times smaller than a human hair. The RNA, which is negatively charged, may have been pulled into the positively charged bubbles in the water.

A 2022 experiment found that when a coacervate bubble floated in a liquid with a bunch of RNA in it, the amount of RNA inside the bubble became about 4,000 times more concentrated than the rest of the RNA floating outside the bubble. The bubbles, it seemed, had a knack for getting lots of genetic material packed inside of them.

In addition to grabbing their own RNA, these bubbles might have also dragged in amino acids, proteins, enzymes, and all sorts of gnarly bits and pieces that would later come together to make more elaborate cells. At this point, they had everything they needed to build a stable place for the RNA to grow and multiply.

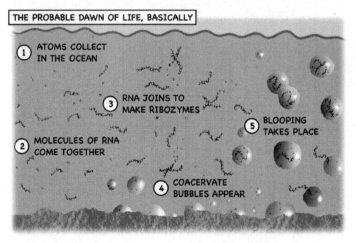

THE PROBABLE DAWN OF LIFE, BASICALLY

1. ATOMS COLLECT IN THE OCEAN
2. MOLECULES OF RNA COME TOGETHER
3. RNA JOINS TO MAKE RIBOZYMES
4. COACERVATE BUBBLES APPEAR
5. BLOOPING TAKES PLACE

As exciting as it is to imagine all of this happening four billion years ago, keep in mind that we've only seen it happen in a lab. The rest is still theoretical, so take it all with a grain of salt. Or salt water, for that matter.

If these bubbles grabbed their own RNA, then life would've made it to Step Two.

GOING FROM CELLS TO PEOPLE

As soon as these basic bubbles started dividing, the real fun began. Chemistry had finally produced a basic unit of life, and there were trillions of them. RNA had cracked the code on how to copy and paste itself over and over again. If the early oceans and hot springs of Earth were teeming with bubbles of RNA, then the entire future of life on Earth depended on one single resource: nucleotides, the building blocks of RNA.

This worked great, until all the nucleotides in a small area were used up. With a limited supply, it was a matter of life and death. The game changed instantly.

❖ RACING TO SURVIVE

Any molecule of RNA that couldn't grab its materials fast enough was beaten by the other molecules that *could*, and so the slower molecules never had the resources to make copies of themselves. The molecules of RNA that *were* fast enough to grab the nucleotides ended up making copies of themselves, and so the next generation of RNA molecules were all faster, stronger, and better at grabbing nucleotides.

At some point, a strand of RNA had a random mutation that caused it to turn into the double-stranded DNA that we all know and love. That mutation gave it a huge advantage over the others: DNA had a more stable type of sugar bond, it could grow longer strands, and it made fewer mistakes when it copied itself. All these benefits made it more capable of surviving in the water without breaking apart. Now DNA was the one vibing and thriving, not RNA.

The reason why DNA beat RNA in the race of life is because it was a *catalyst*: it made the process of copying *way* more efficient, fast, and reliable. It wasn't needed to get life going, but once it evolved, it took over because of how effective it was.

If you need to tell your friend an important message, you could either walk to their place and tell them in-person, or you could give them a call on the phone. One of those options is definitely easier, but both of them work; the phone is just a catalyst.

That's the very basis of how we got from basic cells to people. With competitors always randomly evolving faster and more efficient ways to make copies of themselves, you had to keep up. In this cycle, new pieces constantly fell into place. The first cell to randomly grow a wall around it—a cell membrane—would have been way more effective at keeping its DNA safe than the open and exposed cells around it.

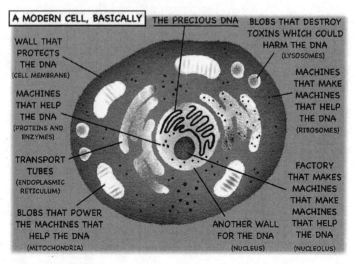

A MODERN CELL, BASICALLY

THE PRECIOUS DNA

BLOBS THAT DESTROY TOXINS WHICH COULD HARM THE DNA (LYSOSOMES)

WALL THAT PROTECTS THE DNA (CELL MEMBRANE)

MACHINES THAT HELP THE DNA (PROTEINS AND ENZYMES)

TRANSPORT TUBES (ENDOPLASMIC RETICULUM)

BLOBS THAT POWER THE MACHINES THAT HELP THE DNA (MITOCHONDRIA)

MACHINES THAT MAKE MACHINES THAT HELP THE DNA (RIBOSOMES)

FACTORY THAT MAKES MACHINES THAT MAKE MACHINES THAT HELP THE DNA (NUCLEOLUS)

ANOTHER WALL FOR THE DNA (NUCLEUS)

The evolution of life is an endless struggle of information trying to stay alive. All the strands of DNA had long strings of information that were coded for certain organisms to grow. If the organism could reproduce fast enough, before it was eaten or beaten by the other organisms around it, then it'd make a copy of its genetic code. If it couldn't reproduce in time, it would die and all the information in its DNA would be erased.

You know you're going to die, but if you choose to make a baby, you've taken your genetic information and copied it into something that'll live longer than you. You've kept your information alive after you die. That's the game of life.

❖ SURVIVAL OF THE FITTEST

When we talk about evolution, the phrase that comes to mind is "survival of the fittest." There are several problems with this phrase, but since it had such a good ring to it, naturally, it was passed on the most effectively, becoming the most popular way to describe evolution.

The reason why "survival of the fittest" doesn't fully describe evolution is because it's not actually about being the strongest or the best; it's about being the most well prepared to reproduce. That means you have to be adaptable.

When DNA is copied, mistakes are made extremely often. A 2010 study in the *National Library of Medicine* found that when our DNA is copied, a mistake is made about once every 10,000 nucleotides. In other words, one in every 10,000 rungs of the DNA ladder is the wrong one. Given how many rungs there are in our entire genetic code, that means there are about a million errors in every single cell every time it makes a copy of itself.

That sounds bad, but it's thanks to these mistakes that we exist.

If our DNA were flawless, it wouldn't have ever made any mistakes; it wouldn't have changed at all, or mutated, since it first appeared nearly four billion years ago. We'd still be living as basic bacteria.

The fact that DNA *isn't* the strongest thing was actually a *greater* benefit to its survival than being flawless. The reason is simple: if *you* aren't able to change, you're going to be destroyed the first time the *environment* changes in a huge way. That's some pretty good life advice from DNA right there.

If you wait long enough, there are going to be rare strokes of good luck—or misfortune, for that matter—that change the whole environment and absolutely demolish the dominant form of life. Just ask the dinosaurs; they know what a sudden change in the environment feels like.

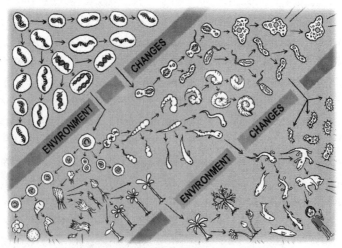

EVOLUTION, WAY TOO OVERSIMPLIFIED.

It's not just asteroid impacts, though. The very reason our cells are so efficient is because of a friendship that arose about two billion years ago. It was a friendship that *no one* could have predicted.

❖ CELLULAR TEAMWORK

Back in the day, 2,000,000,000 years ago, cells were pretty well developed, but they still struggled with the need for more energy. Moving around was tiring, and as cells used valuable energy to break down chemicals, copy their DNA, and dart around the ocean, they had very little power left in reserve.

Somewhere in the ocean, however, a small cell was eaten by another cell and *not* instantly devoured like most of the others. The meal would have been tasty, but we should be thankful it didn't happen; we wouldn't exist otherwise.

Instead, the smaller cell began to live and thrive inside the larger cell. With a safe home, the smaller cell didn't need to spend power on moving around and avoiding being eaten; it could put all its energy toward making more energy. Consequently, the larger cell didn't need to spend its energy digesting its food; it could leave that task to the smaller cell, and devote all its energy to searching for more food to eat. The larger cell ate chemicals, and the smaller cell turned them into energy.

This lucrative process was described in a 2006 paper in *Proceedings of the Royal Society* as "intracellular enslavement," but I respectfully beg to differ. The greatest high school biology meme in history—*mitochondria is the powerhouse of the cell*—was born at that historic moment, two billion years ago.

Working together, both cells got a huge advantage. The smaller cell—which became the mitochondria in our cells today—was safely protected from predators, and the larger cell had a cheap source of energy. The genetic code of the mitochondria was able to copy itself more effectively because it wasn't at risk of being eaten. The genetic code of the larger host cell was able to survive more easily now that it didn't have to scavenge for food all the time.

This made both of them far more efficient at reproducing, and they quickly became the dominant type of cell. Every complex life form on this planet can trace its lineage right back to that moment.

Mitochondria still have their own DNA, even as they live and thrive inside our body cells today. They can divide and multiply, even if our *own* cells aren't dividing. We quite literally have a separate strain of life living inside each of our cells. In a literal sense, we've all had a bacterial infection for the last two billion years!

❖ THE GROUP HUG

Until around two billion years ago, cells went solo. Survival was a matter of reproducing on your own and avoiding being eaten by someone else. But as cells became more developed and began to grow in groups, the concept of *specialization* came along.

Instead of a cell going through the hassle of doing everything on its own—moving, consuming food, making energy, growing, dividing—cells began to work together, taking on tasks that helped each of them survive. It was just like a group project—or, at least, how a group project is supposed to be.

A large group of cells living and working together each have a better chance of survival than they would if they were alone. They're all more likely to pass on their *own* genetic code if they team up and survive with other cells that each want to pass on *their* genetic code.

In that way, the cells in your body aren't really working to keep *you* alive, but rather working to keep the other cells of your body alive, since they're being kept alive by the countless other cells in your body. Everything you do is a real team effort—even if you're working alone.

From two billion years ago and onward, the main race in evolution became which strand of DNA could program cells to grow together in the way that made all of them collectively the best at reproducing.

This competition led to an amazing range of DNA-copying styles. Spores, seeds, and pollen were adapted by plants. As DNA evolved, it became better at growing huge colonies of cells that had special cells *devoted* to making more colonies of cells; it evolved the sperm and the egg. Animals began to evolve.

❖ FOR THE GREATER GOOD

As multicellular life evolved, it forced cells to gain a kind of empathy for other cells. Even though the cells had no thoughts or feelings, they were forced to learn teamwork and sharing, and unlearn the billions of years of "kill everyone else to stay alive" that had been programmed into the way they behaved.

In colonies of yeast, for example, each cell makes a special type of enzyme called amylase, which breaks down starches into simple sugars that all the yeast cells in the colony can eat more easily. When all the cells make amylase, everyone benefits in a real team effort.

But if every yeast cell in a colony does this, then some cells might choose to be lazy and slack off. It would be better for a single yeast cell's own survival to stop making amylase and put its energy toward its own growth instead. It'd still get all the amylase it needed from its neighbours, which practically gave it a free pass.

That works fine for *one* cell, but if too many cells attempt to cheat the system, the whole yeast colony falls apart. It's like a disastrous middle school group project; it all goes down in flames. Over time, then, only the colonies that have devoted cells—cells that are hard-wired to help the collective group and not themselves—will survive in the game of life.

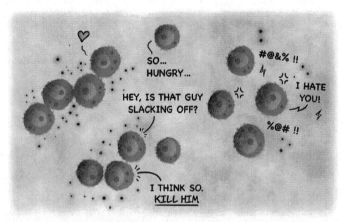

GROUP PROJECTS WERE A LOT DEADLIER BACK THEN.

This dependency was critical to preventing cells from being selfish and trying to cheat the system. For example, mitochondria today literally can't survive outside of the protection of our cells. The host cells would die quickly without the energy from the mitochondria. If either one betrays the other, it's certain death for both of them. Our cells evolved a really selfless code in their DNA: a gene called P53.

If one of our cells has a mutation that could cause it to damage the cells around it, the gene P53 is literally programmed to make the cell commit suicide, blowing itself to bits by releasing little wrecking balls, called caspaces, that rip the cell to shreds.

That process, called apoptosis, seems like a terrible idea when the goal is to pass on your genetic code. But in organisms where no cell ever killed itself, the malfunctioning cells might have turned into cancer and killed the whole organism—taking *every* cell down with it—before the organism as a whole was able to reproduce. Over time, the organisms that had a cell kill-code survived and reproduced more than the organisms that didn't. Cell teamwork was enforced in a really brutal way.

It's like they say in the movies: it's for the greater good.

When you think about it, cancer cells are just ordinary cells that are still hard-wired to put their own survival first. They have their own DNA, their own genetic code, and their own purpose to keep that genetic code in existence for as long as possible.

In a complex organism like the human body, most cells can only survive thanks to other cells.

The neurons in your brain need oxygen to survive, which comes from red blood cells in your bloodstream, which is pumped by the contracting cardiomyocyte cells in your heart, which are sustained with oxygen from the alveoli in your lungs, which, to breathe, require a signal from the neurons in your brain. That signal is usually automatic, but now you're consciously aware of your breathing. You're welcome.

❖ HOW WE GOT TO BE SO SMART

As Neil deGrasse Tyson mentions in Cosmos, Possible Worlds, the story of our evolution has one last absurd stroke of luck: our big brains.

Our brains grew to their full size around two million years ago, when the neocortex—the part of our brain involved in deep thinking and cognition—suddenly expanded. You might expect that such a dramatic change may have been caused by a huge shift in the environment, our whole genome, or our entire species.

Actually, it was a little less dramatic. A research study published in 2016 from the Max Planck Institute of Molecular Cell Biology and Genetics in Germany suggested that we owe our large brains to *one* single gene mutation.

Based on the study, the sudden growth of the neocortex was thanks to a single rung of our DNA ladder being knocked out. A cytosine molecule was smashed out of our genetic code and accidentally replaced by a guanine molecule. That was it! The mutated DNA controlled a special type of protein whose role was to control the growth of cells in the neocortex of our brain. Thanks to the mutation, the protein changed its role: it accelerated the division of cells in the neocortex, making it grow ever faster.

The world was never the same again.

When you think about it, the 8.7 million species that currently live on Earth are all made of the same genetic code: DNA. Is it really a race between different species, or is it all just DNA versus DNA? In a wacky sort of meta-evolution, perhaps the entire history of life on Earth was a method by which one type of molecule, DNA, became as indestructible as possible.

THE ORIGINS OF LIFE ELSEWHERE

Our planet was a molten hellscape after its collision with Theia and the formation of the Moon, and it remained a molten mess for around 500 million years. But life on Earth seemed to materialize and get going a hundred million years after our planet cooled off, which leaves a *very* small window of time for all the necessary building blocks of life to become available.

Life has never ceased to amaze us, so there's no reason to assume it didn't all happen extremely fast. But maybe it's a hint of something else. Perhaps we need to consider another theory, popularized by the astronomer Fred Hoyle in the 1970s, known as *panspermia*. If we want to look for our own origins, we might just be looking on the wrong planet.

YOU KNOW, WE COULD REALLY USE A HITCHHIKER'S GUIDE TO THIS GALAXY.

❖ THE CASE FOR MARS

Around 4.5 billion years ago, Mars likely had oceans of liquid water spanning most of its surface, while at the same time, the Earth had just been rammed by Theia and was completely dead. Shorelines and rivers are still visible on Mars' surface today, and based on a 2022 study out of the University of Copenhagen, those oceans may have been around 300 metres deep, containing all the necessary components for life as we know it. Mars used to be the wet planet, not the red one.

Mars also once had a thicker atmosphere; it could've been up to half as thick as our own atmosphere *currently* is. During that era of the solar system, right at the end of the giant hailstorm of asteroids and comets in the Late Heavy Bombardment, Mars would have received the same chemical treatment as the Earth did, with cosmic rocks raining amino acids and raw elements to the surface.

Even though the distant Sun was dimmer back then, Mars had a huge amount of carbon dioxide in its skies, trapping the heat. If any organisms evolved there, they would have had a billion years to evolve before Mars cooled off.

Eventually, the metallic core of Mars cooled down, causing its magnetic field to fall apart, which let deadly solar radiation strip away the atmosphere. The fallen pressure caused the oceans to boil away, leaving behind only a thin veil of carbon dioxide and a desert of sand dunes.

But interestingly, there have been nearly 300 meteorite discoveries on Earth that originated from Mars, blasted away by asteroid collisions and flung across the void of space to our home planet. Over the entire history of the solar system, if Mars used to be habitable billions of years ago, we could imagine a sort of planetary cross-breeding taking place. Maybe we're all Martians. Or maybe not.

❖ THE CASE FOR VENUS

On the other side of the Earth's orbit, the planet Venus also may have had a brief period of habitability before it became the awful, scorched, corroded, pressure-cooked planet it is today. In 2016, a hypothesis in *Geophysical Research Letters* argued that Venus may have been the first planet in our solar system infected with the disease of life.

It likely had oceans and a mild environment for up to three billion years, in which temperatures ranged from a high of 50°C to a low of 15°C. That's not bad at all!

With all the basic building blocks needed to start an ecosystem, Venus could have thrived and prospered in the first few billion years of the solar system. During the hailstorm of the Late Heavy Bombardment, collisions on Venus could have blasted life-ridden chunks of rock to Earth just as the storm ended, seeding our planet with life.

For a while, it's possible that both Venus *and* Earth were habitable at the same time—until about 700 million years ago. Venus, for some reason, broke. It was smothered in carbon dioxide and turned into the roasting oven that it is today. As its oceans evaporated from intense sunlight, a thick layer of water vapour coated the planet and trapped the Sun's heat, boiling more water and trapping even more heat—a *runaway* greenhouse effect.

Another theory suggests Venus might have been cooked thanks to a shake-up and shattering of the entire surface. Who knows what crazy geological event might have caused this. When the surface cracked and reorganized, it exposed carbon dioxide that had been trapped under the crust. Or maybe it was a huge asteroid that shattered the surface. Perhaps the very same asteroid that blasted chunks of life from Venus to Earth. In that case, no guilt, and no regrets.

❖ A LONG WAYS AWAY

Some studies think that panspermia would take far too long, and that the deadly solar radiation would cook and destroy the genetic code of the microbes. Based on a panspermia analysis in 1997, it could take up to 14 million years for pieces of rock to randomly collide with Earth after being blasted off a nearby planet. They estimated that only 0.006% of the genome would survive the voyage without being baked to a crisp. A harsh commute, that's for sure.

But some bacteria are shockingly resilient. In 2015, an experiment placed bacteria on the outside of the International Space Station, leaving them open to the deadly environment of deep space for three years. One species, *Deinococcus radiodurans*, survived just fine.

In late 2017, an asteroid called Oumuamua zipped through the solar system at such a high speed that it couldn't have possibly come from *inside* our solar system; we had just found the first known visitor from interstellar space.

Ever since we discovered these cosmic trespassers, we've kept finding them. Now it's believed that around *seven* interstellar asteroids are hurtling through our solar system every single year. Could microbes have ferried their way across the absurdly huge voids between stars, seeding our planet with a strain of life that came from outside the solar system?

The further out we extend the possibilities of our origins, the harder it is to answer the simple question of where we came from. Does that obscurity make it more intimidating—or more exciting?

THE STORY OF YOUR ATOMS

You're a traveller. Everyone on this planet—even those who hate vacations—is a cosmic traveller trekking across the cosmos for billions of years.

If the elements of the cosmos were an artist's palette, hydrogen would be the primary colour. All the other atoms in your body were made by smashing lots of hydrogen together. The hydrogen atoms in your body are originals; they came together about 380,000 years after the Big Bang, and they haven't changed since.

❖ COOKED IN A STAR

The other elements in your body, such as carbon, nitrogen, and phosphorous, were smashed together at the centres of red giant stars.

At their cores, the mad pinball of nuclear fusion constantly smashed hydrogen together into heavier atoms. As the stars grew older, helium atoms were smashed together into carbon, carbon was smashed into oxygen, and so on. When each star finally died, it blasted its innards throughout the cosmos, creating a dazzling planetary nebula.

In the hot cores of billions of stars across the universe, this cascade of atom-smashing was happening all the time. Stars were all you needed to bake most of the elements up to oxygen. For the larger atoms, you needed a bigger furnace.

All of the metals around you were first cooked in the most colossal forges in the universe: red supergiant stars.

The sizes of these things were absolutely absurd. If you swapped the Sun out for an average red supergiant, the orbits of Jupiter and Saturn would be inside it.

At the very middle of these behemoth stars, atoms were slammed into each other, from neon into oxygen, from oxygen into silicon, and lastly from silicon into iron. When atoms were fused together, a huge amount of energy was released. That surge of energy blasted the star's layers outward, pushing against the massive gravity crushing inward.

However, heavier atoms were harder for the star to fuse, since they required more energy to smash together and didn't give off as much energy when they fused. When the star began fusing *iron*, the amount of energy gotten out of the reaction was finally *less* than the energy put into it. The enormous burning furnace lost its power. The reaction died. The huge pull of gravity, with no explosion left to push against it, caused the whole star to collapse in on itself.

When a red supergiant collapses, it's a bit like taking two cymbals and smashing them together. Except, of course, each cymbal is glowing at about 1,000,000,000°C and weighs as much as 3,000,000 Earths. As the cymbals crash together at a quarter of the *speed of light*, it's one heck of a boom, to say the least. The whole star, which may have weighed around 10–20 times as much as the Sun, crunches down at about 75,000 kilometres per second. Then, the whole thing rebounds and blows up in a supernova. The explosion is so utterly colossal that it blasts more energy in a couple of seconds than our Sun will emit over its entire ten-billion-year lifespan.

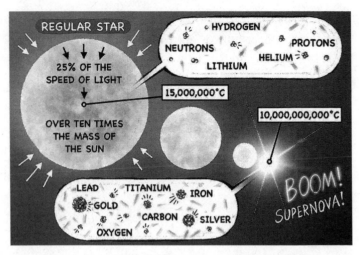

At the centre of this mayhem, it becomes so absurdly hot that atoms of iron are easily smashed together into heavier and heavier elements such as uranium, gold, platinum, tungsten, lead, and dozens of other metals.

About 2.5% of your body is made of metals, which means around 175 million million million million atoms in your body were cooked in distant supernova explosions, billions of years ago. As much as you may not like it, you're a metal fan.

The supernova blasted these metals into the galaxy. For a while, it glowed as a spectacular nebula. Then it faded into a dark dust cloud that mixed into the swirling whirlpool of our galaxy. One of these clouds is the one that our solar system came from. The cloud collapsed under its weak gravity, and in the middle, it got so hot and dense that a star ignited. The Sun was born.

Just think of the stupendous odds that *all* your atoms of metal made in supernova explosions across the cosmos, your atoms of oxygen and carbon forged in the cores of dying stars, and your atoms of hydrogen produced less than a million years after the Big Bang itself—*all* randomly came to the exact same place at the same time in cosmic history, making a brief collection of stardust: you.

THE UNIVERSE IS BORN

The farther out we look into space, the further back into time we are seeing. Because it takes light longer to reach us, we are peering into the distant past. Eventually, we can't even see galaxies anymore because galaxies simply didn't exist that far in the past.

If we had powerful enough eyes, you might think we'd be able to see right back to the birth of the universe itself. Except we can't, because light couldn't shine across our cosmos until around 380,000 years after the Big Bang, when the dense clouds of gas left over from the Big Bang finally cleared up.

❖ THE COSMIC MICROWAVE BACKGROUND

The oldest light in the universe is a faint aura of microwave radiation known as the *Cosmic Microwave Background.* It's like the home screen wallpaper of our cosmos, showing an image of our universe so far in the past that atoms hadn't even bonded to make molecules yet. Planets and stars didn't exist, and atoms themselves were fresh out of the oven.

The early universe was filled with hot plasma, and it would've been filled with gamma radiation. But due to the universe's expansion since then, those gamma rays have been stretched and lengthened into faint microwaves. The Cosmic Microwave Background is basically our universe's baby ultrasound image, made of the first light that leaked out from the gaseous maelstrom of the early universe.

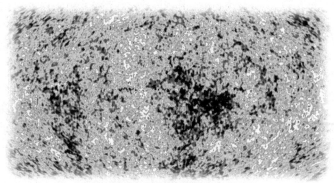

OUR UNIVERSE'S FIRST BABY PHOTO

By definition, that makes the Cosmic Microwave Background the first official "leaked" photo in the universe.

The Cosmic Microwave Background is still out there, saturating our universe with faint radiation leftover from the Big Bang itself. Some of the static you see on an untuned television screen is that distant radiation interfering with its antenna. Even a household television can show you the afterglow of the birth of the entire universe. The static noise that comes from an untuned television is, in a small part, the audio version of the Big Bang; it's truly the first radio channel ever broadcast on live television.

The Cosmic Microwave Background is the absolute limit of what we can see, since no light from beyond that point can reach us, and we reluctantly are forced to drop the camera. But we can still speculate on what happened before then using two other hints. Frankly, the baby scan of our universe was a little odd.

❖ TOO TEMPERATE AND FLAT

The temperature of our early universe was almost exactly the same everywhere. The bright spots in the Cosmic

Microwave Background were the hottest places in the early universe, and the dark spots were the coolest places, but they only varied in temperature by about 1/5000th of a degree. If this doesn't immediately sound weird to you, picture a version of our world where the hot beaches in Hawaii, the ice sheets in Antarctica, the tropical rainforests in Brazil, the polar north in Canada, the sauna at your local gym, the ice cream at the store, and the water you drink are all exactly the same temperature. This problem was first discovered in 1956 by theoretical physicist Wolfgang Rindler, and it was called the *Horizon Problem*.

The second problem was this: the universe's curvature is known to be almost completely flat. This doesn't make much sense in our universe, especially given how old it is. Picture the universe's curvature like a pencil balanced on its tip, which, when nudged in a particular direction, falls at a quickening pace in that direction. If our universe began to develop any sort of curvature, it would have curved at a quickening pace until it curled up completely. But our cosmos still appears to be flat and have zero curvature.

The chances of that happening are pretty slim, since our universe has had nearly fourteen billion years to teeter off perfect flatness and fall into a curved shape. Imagine a pencil that has been standing on its tip for fourteen billion years. This problem is known as the *Flatness Problem*.

How do astronomers and cosmologists grapple with these problems? The best-known interpretation solving both the Flatness Problem and the Horizon Problem suggests that our universe blew up in the beginning.

"But wait," you might interject, "don't we already *know* that the universe blew up in the beginning?" To put things in perspective, if the Big Bang sounded like an impressive spectacle, it's nothing when put against the event that likely happened just before it, known as *cosmic inflation*. It was the biggest boom in cosmic history.

❖ THE BIGGER BANG

In the early 1980s, the theoretical physicists and cosmologists Alan Guth, Alexei Starobinsky, and Andrei Linde worked on solving the origins of our universe. The solution they established suggests that the universe didn't explode into existence as a fireball of plasma, but actually first began with no matter or heat at all—just an empty void of space.

This eerie period of time was like a cosmic dark age. It only lasted for ten billionths of a trillionth of a trillionth of a second, but in that tiny sliver of time, a lot happened.

While space was devoid of matter and energy, it had a mysterious force that blew the universe apart at unimaginable speeds and expanded it to astronomical size. The newborn cosmos exploded, then grew in size by one hundred million million million million times in a mere fraction of a second. During this cosmic inflation, our universe was out of control. Space was violently stretched from subatomic to intergalactic scale.

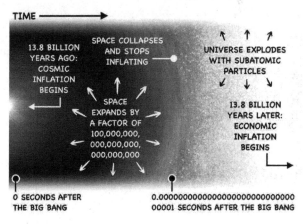

TIME ⟶

13.8 BILLION YEARS AGO: COSMIC INFLATION BEGINS

SPACE COLLAPSES AND STOPS INFLATING

UNIVERSE EXPLODES WITH SUBATOMIC PARTICLES

SPACE EXPANDS BY A FACTOR OF 100,000,000,000,000,000,000,000,000

13.8 BILLION YEARS LATER: ECONOMIC INFLATION BEGINS

0 SECONDS AFTER THE BIG BANG

0.00000000000000000000000000000 00001 SECONDS AFTER THE BIG BANG

Imagine a blueberry expanding to the size of our galaxy in less time than it takes a beam of light to cross the width of a human hair.

After this brief flurry, inflation ended, space finally calmed down, and the universe as we know it came into existence. Why do we suspect that something so crazy actually happened? The two prominent problems with our universe's current baby image—the fact that it was almost exactly the same temperature everywhere, and that it was too perfectly flat—are both solved if we accept this theory.

Since the newborn cosmos expanded far faster than the speed of light, no objects would have been able to transfer heat to any other object; nothing can transmit anything faster than light, which kept the temperature about the same everywhere. Also, if our universe had any curvature to begin with, it expanded so absurdly fast that the curvature was stretched into a nearly flat universe. Problems solved.

If this is the origin of our universe, it's strange why inflation ever stopped at all. Since the universe had such a powerful force driving space apart in all directions, it's fortunate, for our sake, that it suddenly slowed down and settled into a more steady state—one that expands slow enough to allow for galaxies and stars, planets and chemistry, and eventually life. But what exactly *caused* the universe to settle down?

THE ORIGIN OF EVERYTHING

One of the greatest contributors to a physicist's existential dread is a process known as *vacuum decay*. It's a problem that's so deeply entrenched into the laws of physics that there isn't anything we can do to stop it, but which would be so catastrophic that it would erase the entire cosmos from existence.

A basic rule in our universe is that objects tend toward their lowest energy state. In other words, any object that contains energy will eventually find a way to lose that energy. Hot metal transfers its heat into the surrounding air until it reaches a stable temperature; pendulums swing until they lose their energy and come to a stop; a ball on the top of a hill will roll down until it reaches flat ground. The mystery here, in a deeper sense, is whether space itself might follow this rule too.

❖ SPACE COLLAPSES

If space contains a lot of extra energy, it seems to be possible that it could suddenly collapse into a more stable version of space, instantly losing that extra energy in the process. If this is true, then we're living in something called a *false vacuum*. If space were to collapse, it would permanently alter the laws of physics and produce a violently expanding sphere of stable space that would grow at the speed of light and dissolve the entire universe. To add to the existential angst, anything travelling at the speed of light is completely invisible until it arrives, so we would have no way to see it coming, even if it were five seconds away from annihilating our planet and everyone on it.

When our universe was in its brief period of cosmic inflation, it contained a stupendous amount of extra energy, causing it to expand almost instantly from subatomic to galactic sizes. This sort of space would've been extremely unstable, and likely quickly collapsed into a more stable form of space, something like the space that we now inhabit.

However, when space decays into a more stable form of space, it's like throwing a boulder off a cliff into the more stable valley below; it doesn't just quietly happen, but instead releases a huge amount of energy in the process. Physicists believe that in the moments right after space collapsed, an unimaginable amount of energy was released—enough to cook everything in our universe to about 100,000,000,000,000,000,000,000,000,000,000°C. You don't think you're hot? Think again.

If you pack a huge amount of energy into a small space, you'll start to trigger all sorts of wacky and exciting quantum effects. When objects are heated up to mind-boggling temperatures, particles of matter and antimatter start popping out of the mixture of pure energy. You literally start getting solid matter out of nothing but energy.

In 2021, the Brookhaven National Laboratory managed to blast pairs of electron and positron particles out of pure nothingness, simply by colliding two high-energy beams of light.

In the newborn universe, space was so unbelievably energetic and hot that weird quantum stuff happened *everywhere*. In an instant, all the excess heat in the cosmos turned into a primordial soup of matter and antimatter, seeding the universe with the particles that would one day become stars, planets, and eventually us.

When inflation ended and our universe was converted to a hot mixture of particles, it was still about the size of a tennis ball. Then something amazing happened: tiny subatomic particles popped in and out of existence, and as they did, they left little blemishes and pockmarks in our baby universe. When our cosmos expanded to billions of light-years in size, those subatomic pockmarks were stretched to intergalactic distances. Those slight cosmic blemishes created hot spots and cool spots, which eventually formed clumps of matter, which led to the formation of galaxies, stars, planets, and life.

The cosmic web of galaxies, and all the structure we see in the current cosmos, can be traced back to the tiny fingerprints that subatomic particles left on the universe when it was smaller than an atom and less than a nanosecond old.

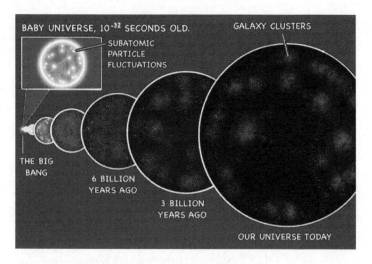

BABY UNIVERSE, 10^{-32} SECONDS OLD.

SUBATOMIC PARTICLE FLUCTUATIONS

GALAXY CLUSTERS

THE BIG BANG

6 BILLION YEARS AGO

3 BILLION YEARS AGO

OUR UNIVERSE TODAY

❖ THE REVISED ORIGIN STORY

Our cosmic origins are amazing, and so much more complex than just an egg and a sperm coming together. The chemical machines that tick along in our cells probably came from the deep oceans or the smoky clouds on our early Earth, or even from wild comets careening through the solar system.

The atoms that compose our bodies are the products of billions of years of fusion reactions at the cores of stars. The heavier elements are products of those stars undergoing devastatingly beautiful supernova explosions. But those fusion reactions only took particles, moved them around, and squashed them into different atoms; the particles themselves were created in the intense explosion of energy that was released right after the universe was born.

In the very deepest sense, we're a reconfiguration of the explosive energy of the expansion of space itself. That, frankly, is pretty cool.

BEFORE THE BEGINNING

With observations and speculation, we can travel back to the very instant our cosmos exploded into existence. We know that cosmic inflation expanded our universe to an enormous size, and when it finally ended, the extra energy collapsed into the particles that make up our universe today. But a huge mystery is still glaring at us: what happened before cosmic inflation and our universe existed?

If we have the audacity to consider what happened before the Big Bang, would we expect to find some earlier and bigger bang, or is it possible that time has existed forever without any official beginning? Cosmologists struggled enough just to determine whether *space* was finite or infinite, and similarly, they were confronted with the same problem for *time*: either time suddenly began at some point, or it has existed forever.

In 1986, the American physicist Andrei Linde explored the second option, developing a hypothesis called *eternal inflation*. In that hypothesis, he presumed that time had been going on forever, stretching endlessly into the past and future. Based on this idea, our grandiose Big Bang isn't really so big after all, and it isn't much of a bang either. Linde's hypothesis supposes that cosmic inflation is happening all the time—even right now as you read this.

❖ ETERNAL INFLATION HYPOTHESIS

Picture an endless void of complete darkness. Everywhere around you, space is inflating rapidly, growing trillions of times larger every second. Occasionally, a brief flash momentarily lights up the darkness before it fades into the distance. These flashes occur all around you, pitting the blackness with sparks.

This idea might sound haunting, but perhaps space looked like that before our universe was born, will look like that after it dies, and looks like that even now at this very moment—outside of our universe.

Because this endless void of space is inflating and expanding so fast, it exists in a false vacuum, containing a huge amount of energy that's ready to suddenly collapse at any moment. Those collapses happen across the cosmos at random, like lone fireworks going off in an endless sea of blackness. The collapses in space lead to their own little "pocket universes" appearing, just like our own universe, out of the endless riptide of inflation.

For every second that inflation ticks onward, trillions of random collapses trigger trillions of new pocket universes all over the place—all sharing a similar origin story to our own universe. All of them are born out of pure luck and random chance. But don't get too excited about the prospect of visiting those distant universes; the space in between them is still inflating as usual, pushing us and them trillions of times further away each second.

Even if we're effectively isolated in our own pocket universe, it's profoundly awesome to know that new universes are spawning every single second. Even cooler, those distant universes won't necessarily have the same laws of physics.

Remember how the sudden collapse of inflating space is like throwing a boulder from a cliff down into a stable valley? In that analogy, there's nothing saying the boulder *has* to roll all the way to the bottom—it just has to roll until it finds a new stable location. Perhaps it lands on a ledge that's still thousands of feet off the ground. The point is, when space collapses, it doesn't always settle with *our* kind of universe—it could settle on something completely different.

There could be universes being born at this very moment where gravity behaves very differently. Perhaps some universes have a different speed of light, some have no magnetic forces holding atoms together, some might have heavier particles that destroy that universe, some might have different laws of atomic physics that make nuclear fusion impossible, and some might instantly collapse on themselves.

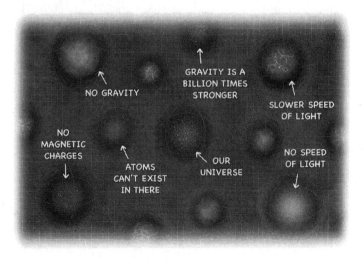

❖ A MAGICAL MIRACLE

Our universe has many laws of physics that seem to be amazing coincidences. The Strong Nuclear Force holding atoms together, is just strong enough to sustain nuclear fusion inside stars, powering them and making them shine. If the Strong Nuclear Force had been 1/25th stronger, it would've made fusion too powerful, making every star in the universe blow up like a nuclear bomb, killing all the planets in an instant.

If protons had been even 1/500th heavier than they are in this universe, they would have instantly decayed and dissolved into other subatomic particles, destroying every little bit of matter in the entire universe.

Gravity is the force that pulls objects together in space, while *dark energy*—which we'll look at in the next chapter—is the force that pushes space apart. Both of those forces are perfectly balanced between pushing apart and pulling together, keeping our universe stable. If these two forces were even 1 part in 10^{120} (that's a 1 followed by 120 zeroes) stronger or weaker than they currently are, our universe would have destroyed itself a long time ago. So many fantastic coincidences are found in our universe that we could easily conclude it was serendipitously meant to be. We might believe that we're somehow magically and perfectly made for this universe. If you feel the same way, you've got a sensible case of the *anthropic bias*.

If you look at every possible universe and every possible version of the laws of physics, chances are you won't find life in most of them. In universes where the speed of light is zero, nothing ever happens, so no life. In universes where gravity pushes outward instead of pulling inward, planets and stars never come together, so no life. In universes where atoms can't form, there's no life. If atoms can't bond with each other and create chemistry, there's no life. Most of the other universes out there are probably dead and lifeless. Nobody lives in them, nobody really cares about them, and nobody sits in those universes thinking deeply about their existence or the meaning of life.

In order for life to exist, it needs laws of physics that allow life to exist. Duh.

But do we really need a *reason* to find ourselves in this amazingly rare universe? If the laws of physics had been any different, we wouldn't have existed in the first place, so you definitely wouldn't be sitting around reading this book or questioning your life and existence.

At the risk of stating the obvious, if this particular universe allows for life as we know it, we shouldn't expect to find ourselves in any universe other than this one. The real reason we originated from this perfect universe isn't because it was meant to be, but rather because biochemistry worked in this universe and clearly didn't in the others.

Or perhaps it did, and that led to the amazing possibility of exotic life under different laws of physics. If intelligent civilizations ever existed in far-off universes with crazy laws of physics, they, too, might make the mistake of romanticizing their universe as a perfect stroke of serendipity.

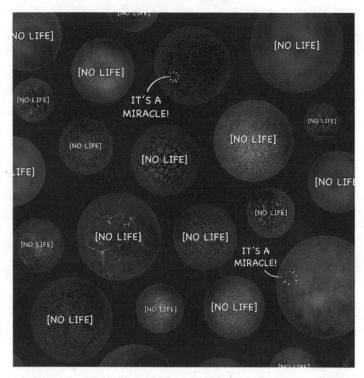

However distant and foreign they are to us, we cannot even begin to imagine what their cosmos would be like—and in the time it took you to read this sentence, the unstoppable expansion of cosmic inflation has pushed them trillions of times further away.

But what an incredible origin story it is for the both of us.

PART 4

THE COSMIC FUTURE

OUR UNIVERSE EXISTS ON
BORROWED TIME

How is everything going to die? On a brighter note, could the universe exist forever? Or will space and time come crashing down in a spectacular grand finale? The possibilities for the future of our universe are truly mind-boggling, from the collapse of everything in existence, to the end of spacetime itself, to entirely new universes spawning from the aftermath of our dead cosmos. ·

But first, a brief note on the apocalypse.

The idea of the end of the world is certainly nothing new. In fact, if every one of the predicted doomsdays within the Christian, Hebrew, Islamic, and Mayan calendars actually came true, our world would have ended over two hundred times by now. While the total destruction of our planet seems pretty bad, the universe would tick onward as usual, and there would still be ten septillion other planets in the cosmos and none of them would notice if our world were to suddenly vanish.

Even if a mere planetary apocalypse isn't so bad in the bigger picture, we live in a universe that is ticking toward a cosmic doomsday. The end of the universe really is a shame, because there won't be a legacy, survivors to tell the story of such-and-such, or any aftermath worth witnessing. The end of the universe is far more sobering than the end of just the Earth. So, without further ado, what events are in store that could destroy the entire universe?

More than you might expect.

THE END OF THE UNIVERSE

The universe is dangerously balanced between safety and certain death. Two powerful forces, both entirely capable of destroying the cosmos on their own, are locked in a cosmic battle for dominance. The deciding factor of our universe's fate will entirely depend on which force wins the battle. Will dark energy take victory, or will gravity assert dominance? Both have their own cosmic doomsdays in store.

❖ DUEL OF THE FORCES

Dark energy is a mysterious force we don't yet understand. With no effect on normal matter other than pushing it apart, dark energy appears to be part of space itself. As space expands, more dark energy is produced, which in turn continues to expand space. Dark energy is the ultimate counterbalance to gravity, relentlessly forcing the universe apart in all directions. It doesn't physically push objects apart, but rather expands space itself, dragging objects along for the ride. If dark energy wins this cosmic battle, it will cause our universe to uncontrollably expand and rip itself to shreds.

In 1998, two teams of astronomers made observations on how quickly distant galaxies were expanding away from us. Much to the surprise of everyone, our cosmos was not only expanding, it was accelerating in its expansion: a runaway cosmos, entirely at the mercy of dark energy, a force which we barely understand.

We have gravity to save the day.

Gravity is a force we routinely encounter. Known for pulling massive objects together, gravity is an attractive force, holding the mass of our planet to itself, locking the Moon in orbit around the Earth, fixing our planet in its dance around the Sun, pushing sleepy people to the ground, and keeping our entire galaxy intact.

However, too much of a good thing could just as easily lead our universe to certain doom; without the help of dark energy pushing our universe apart, gravity would reverse the expansion and hurl our cosmos toward a catastrophic collapse.

In fact, when Einstein was first developing his theory of general relativity, he wondered why our universe hadn't *already* collapsed under gravity. Although he just corrected this problem by adding a cosmological constant pressure to push against gravity, little did he know that he had uncovered the first hints of gravity's deadlock rival: dark energy.

Presently, the clash between gravity and dark energy appears to be an even match. Dark energy is extremely strange, and, given that the fate of our universe rests entirely at its mercy, we seem to be at a loss in figuring out how our cosmos will meet its fate. But we can simplify things a little. Regardless of dark energy's mysteries, it's either going to win this battle, lose it, or keep being in balance.

If dark energy's strength never changes, our universe will stay in a perfect balance forever, sparing it from the chaotic drama of the other two possibilities. If dark energy gets *weaker* over time, it would indicate that it is slowly dispersing itself, and that gravity will win the cosmic battle of doom.

If dark energy becomes *stronger* as time passes, it would indicate that dark energy is becoming denser, saturating the cosmos, and producing more of itself as time ticks on. That would be very bad for us, even by apocalyptic standards.

TWO COSMIC FATES

Suppose that dark energy is getting weaker over time, and gradually spreading itself out as the future goes on. That doesn't necessarily mean we're doomed—not in the immediate sense, anyway. Our universe might keep expanding, but at a slower and slower rate, coming closer and closer to grinding to a halt but never quite stopping. That would be the best possible outcome. The rest is worse.

If dark energy becomes a *lot* weaker in the future, we're in for a serious problem as gravity takes its toll. The future wouldn't leave us in a cold and empty universe— it would result in the exact opposite.

❖ WHERE GRAVITY WINS

The first signs of trouble will take place as our universe's expansion slows down over billions of years, with gravity finally pulling it to a halt. Then, the universe will begin to contract back inward upon itself, causing every galaxy in the cosmos to rush toward every other galaxy at a speedy rate. In the time it would take for this to happen, some very interesting events will occur.

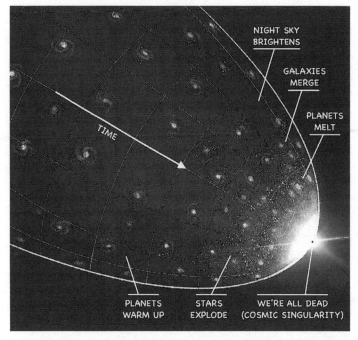

NIGHT SKY
BRIGHTENS

GALAXIES
MERGE

PLANETS
MELT

TIME

PLANETS
WARM UP

STARS
EXPLODE

WE'RE ALL DEAD
(COSMIC SINGULARITY)

First of all, the universe will begin to look a lot brighter.

Currently, the universe is expanding outward, stretching the waves of light that reach us. Today, the most distant galaxies in our universe are receding so fast that their light is stretched and dimmed into an eerie crimson glow. But in the future, if the universe's expansion reverses, those distant galaxies will be rushing toward us at high speed, and the contraction of the universe compresses their light: a reversed version of redshift, called blueshift.

The light from distant galaxies will become compressed into bright blue, violet, and ultraviolet rays. This will treat any surviving life forms to a spectacular night sky filled with a bright blue view of billions of galaxies. On another note, the whole universe will essentially turn into a UV tanning salon.

As the universe continues to collapse, the night sky will get a worse and worse blueshift. Ultraviolet will turn first to X-rays, then gamma rays. Eventually, even the faint background glow of the universe, the Cosmic Microwave Background radiation, will get compressed from long microwave light into shorter and brighter *visible* light. That means, as the universe kept shrinking, the night sky would become a deep red rather than pitch black.

Eventually, as the universe shrinks even more, red light will get compressed into orange, then to yellow, and eventually to all the colours of the rainbow. At some point, about a billion years before the end, our night sky will look like something you might see on an acid trip. It will be a beautiful and trippy sight, especially since we'd be screaming in agony by that point.

❖ THE UNPLEASANT CRUNCH

The ambient temperature of space will also begin to rise in the final billions of years. At the present moment, the universe is –270°C in the middle of empty space, which is absolutely freezing. But in a universe that shrinks in size, the temperature will go up dramatically as things become squeezed together. This will quickly surpass the comfort levels of most people—even the die-hard summer vacationists.

As matter begins to coalesce, heat pockets become more concentrated. Eventually, the ambient temperature of our universe will become warm enough for liquid water to exist—a comfortable temperature in the void of space itself—which would melt all the icy planets drifting through the cosmos. This brief era of cosmic asylum will not last long, although it would surely be an interesting time, in which every single planet in the cosmos briefly becomes habitable.

If life were able to kickstart itself on Earth in a mere hundred million years, then perhaps it could evolve on melting icy planets in this brief window of pleasant heat in a collapsing universe. It's a real shame, then, what happens next.

In just a few million years, the universe's ambient temperature shoots past 100°C and vaporizes every ocean on every watery world throughout the cosmos. As temperatures soar to thousands of degrees, the air boils away, bedrock melts into magma, and planets begin to convert themselves to plasma.

All the light in the universe becomes compressed, turning the cosmos into an endless oven of gamma radiation. In the final few moments before our universe completely collapses, everything merges into one stupendously large black hole, containing all the matter in the universe combined. This is known rather unambiguously as the *Big Crunch*.

Our universe will then fully collapse into an infinitely small point in space: a *cosmic singularity*. It will be an eerie reverse of the Big Bang itself.

While it'd certainly be an epic way to go, the aftermath of the cosmic collapse is still a mystery. Would our universe remain a singularity forever, or would it rebound into a new Big Bang, starting the entire process anew? The second option, known as the *Big Bounce* theory, would have weird implications for us. If our universe could bounce after it collapses, that means it might have already bounced, leading to our own universe. We would be at a loss to describe just how many universes existed before ours. We could be in the tenth cycle, or the trillionth, or even somewhere in the middle of an infinite number of cosmic bounces.

Even if we're headed for a cosmic collapse, the possibility of a cosmic bounce would definitely add some solace to the existential dread.

❖ WHERE DARK ENERGY WINS

If the previous scenario seems unsettling, you haven't considered the second option: perhaps dark energy is actually getting stronger as time passes, expanding space in all directions with more and more power.

In this case, we'd be in even deeper trouble than the previous scenario.

In a dark-energy-dominated universe, space gets blasted apart much quicker, which has bad consequences for anything that prefers to stay in one piece, such as ourselves.

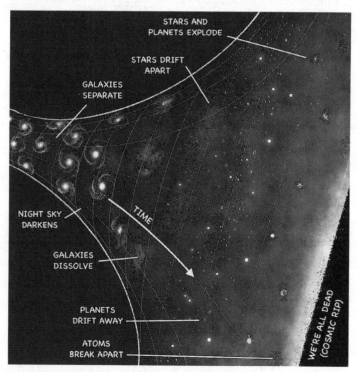

STARS AND
PLANETS EXPLODE

STARS DRIFT
APART

GALAXIES
SEPARATE

NIGHT SKY
DARKENS

TIME

GALAXIES
DISSOLVE

PLANETS
DRIFT AWAY

ATOMS
BREAK APART

WE'RE ALL DEAD
(COSMIC RIP)

As the future unfolds, everything naturally appears okay for the first few billion years, since gravity is stronger at closer distances. Galaxies hold together just fine, but galactic superclusters and the largest structures in the universe will slowly begin to drift apart. The galaxies around the fringes of superclusters will drift away first, then the more central ones, and finally every galaxy. Our Milky Way galaxy will become isolated in its own empty pocket of space.

Such a process will play out incredibly slowly—so slowly that we probably won't see it in action until it is too late. Because we can only see distant galaxies as they appeared in the distant past, by the time we actually begin to see those galaxies disappearing from our vision, we will already be in the thick of our catastrophic doom. In the last few million years, things will get very bad.

❖ THE EPIC GRAND FINALE

Over the span of a few million years, a process known as the *Big Rip* will unfold.

Our own Milky Way galaxy is held together tightly by gravity, but it also contains a tremendous amount of expanding space within it. In a future where dark energy pushes space apart, our galaxy will eventually be pulled apart by the rapid expansion of space itself. Gravity will be too feeble to pull stars back together as space forces them apart.

For the final few thousand years, our sky will be pitch black—a lonely and terrifying reminder of our impending doom, even in the newfound peace and quiet of the expanding cosmos.

Eventually, our solar system will be dragged apart, detaching the outer planets and the asteroids from their orbits around the Sun. Next, Earth will be pulled away, leaving us in complete darkness. For a few hours, perhaps even days, we will be left floating in our own isolated universe. What our society would be doing in that time, I have no clue.

Unfortunately, the peace of the darkness won't persist for very long. The Earth contains space within it, so the Earth itself will eventually begin to expand. Our planet is made of solid rock, so it isn't very stretchable. Crumbling like a dry cookie in all directions, our planet will be ripped to shreds.

In the final seconds, everything happens all at once. All remaining pieces of rock will be ripped into molecules. Then, the expansion of space breaks the chemical bonds between atoms, and molecules would get ripped into individual atoms. In the final fraction of a second, even those atoms will get pulled into individual subatomic particles.

There is no way to survive this cosmic catastrophe. Under the known laws of physics, there's no way to get out of space itself. Better luck next time.

Except, there wouldn't *be* a "next time," since time and space would literally be ripped apart. At time zero, the expansion of space will become infinite. Physics is at a loss to describe exactly what would happen here, and nobody has a clue what would come after it. If you try and plug it in on a calculator, it says you've broken it. All matter will be totally annihilated, and all the particles in the universe will get spread infinitely far apart from each other, never to meet again.

It's like taking a small chunk of butter and spreading it over an infinitely large toast. That's how weird the Big Rip would be. Time and space completely cease to exist. This is the absolute end, not just of the universe, but of reality itself. If your typical apocalypse is "the end," the Big Rip is "*THE END.*"

WHERE THE UNIVERSE BALANCES

By some cosmic miracle, suppose that dark energy doesn't change at all in the future. This amazing fluke would mean that dark energy is a uniform property of space. This would save us from the troubles and woes of a Big Crunch or a Big Rip. The universe would be destined to quietly and calmly exist forever, without any sudden surprises. That leaves us with a very lengthy—and potentially infinite—future in this universe. In this scenario, it won't be space that kills us, but rather a fundamental law of nature known as *entropy*.

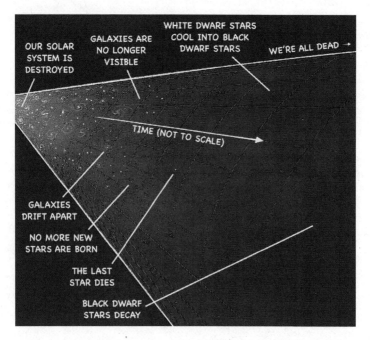

❖ THERMODYNAMIC DOOM

The laws of thermodynamics are the rules that govern how matter and energy move around. You'll have better luck breaking the laws with robbery and fraud than breaking the laws of thermodynamics; there's absolutely no known way of breaking them.

The first law of thermodynamics should really be to *not talk about* the laws of thermodynamics. Sadly, it's not.

The first law is basically this: energy can't be created or destroyed, only moved around. All the energy that was created in the Big Bang is still here, in some form or another. Some of it is moving around as light. Some of it is carried in moving objects. Some of it is stored in electrons as electric power. Some of it is even packed away inside matter, because as Einstein said with $E = mc^2$, all matter is just stored energy. That's the reason why solid particles pop into existence when you blast enough heat and energy into something. The point is, as our universe gets older, it won't lose any energy, it'll just keep moving energy from one place to another.

The second law is this: order and tidiness will always fall apart into disorder and messiness. Everything in the cosmos, all as a whole, will slowly move toward a state of chaos and disorder. As energy moves from one place to another, it always leaves the situation a little more disordered than it was before. That disorder is entropy.

A recently cleaned room is a great analogy of entropy in action: it seems to make a mess of itself without anyone even trying. Similarly, an ordered pair of wired earbuds, left unchecked, somehow gets hundreds of unsolvable knots without any effort. It's not really your fault, but rather a basic law of the universe: entropy.

In addition to creating untidy rooms and tangled ear-buds, entropy is what causes wood to convert to charcoal and release a lot of heat, but at the same time prohibits charcoal from un-burning back into wood and cooling the air down. It's the reason why you can stir a sugar cube into a plain cup of tea to make sugary tea, but you can't stir a sugary cup of tea and produce a sugar cube floating in plain tea.

A little disorder here and there is essential. If the universe never became untidy and disordered, nothing would ever happen. There'd be no crazy collisions, no messy chemical reactions, and no chaotic explosions. The universe would be a totally plain sea of pure and uniform elementary particles.

A little entropy is excellent, since it allows chaotic and messy things like life to occur. However, we are just a temporary phase in the universe's disorder. The cosmos is still getting more disordered, and it certainly won't stop with us.

The reason our universe tends toward disorder is a statistical effect. There are more ways to create a messy situation than a tidy one. As an analogy, if everything in a room belongs in exactly one place, there's exactly one way to make a perfectly tidy room. But there are several million ways to make a messy room by randomly strewing objects across the floor.

Our universe works in the same way; it's tending toward disorder because there are more ways the universe can be messy than it can be tidy. This means certain doom for us, our civilization, our planet, our solar system, our galaxy, and the whole universe.

❖ OUR SOLAR SYSTEM DIES

In a blink of an eye on the cosmic timeline, the Earth will already be gone. Our planet is doomed to a fiery fate within the Sun because it orbits so closely. In around five billion years, our star will exhaust its supply of hydrogen. As the Sun struggles to fuse helium into heavier elements like carbon, its fusion reaction will begin to fizzle out.

When its fusion reaction fades, our Sun will lose its outward-pushing pressure against gravity and collapse inward on itself. The collapse, however, will crush the core and make the plasma burn hotter, fusing heavier elements, pushing outward with even greater pressure, and inflating our star's size tremendously.

Over the timeline of about a billion years, the Sun will go through a series of pulsations, inflating a little larger each time. Mercury and Venus will eventually be engulfed by the bloating outer layers of our star, vaporized, and obliterated. The Sun will keep growing until it reaches its largest size, a swollen ball of plasma around 250 times larger than it is today. That's huge enough, unfortunately, to devour our planet and instantly vaporize it.

A few billion years after consuming the Earth, our Sun will pulse its outer layers into space, creating a bright planetary nebula, and destroy the entire solar system in the process.

In the end, all that will be left of our once-glorious solar system will be a faint and sombre white dwarf star surrounded by a sparse cloud of gas and dust. The blazing remnant of our star will only shine with 1/10,000th of the Sun's current brightness. The average sunny afternoon will be like a gloomy night. The remains of our solar system will be a lonely place, but despite that, the universe will go on. We won't be the showstoppers, and we certainly won't stop the show.

❖ THE STARS FADE AWAY

Galaxies will keep evolving and new stars will continue being born, seemingly as if our solar system never existed in the first place. Even as the universe expands into a larger and emptier state, individual galaxies will hardly change.

While the blazing-hot, sun-like stars will quickly burn out, the fainter red dwarf stars will continue shining for up to a hundred trillion (100,000,000,000,000) years, which is an impressive length of time—seven thousand times longer than the current age of the universe.

Thousands of generations of sun-like stars will pass by before a single red dwarf star goes through its life cycle, allowing cosmic safe havens to persist incredibly far into the future. Planets orbiting red dwarf stars will make ideal long-term habitats for humanity, if we're still around then.

Red dwarf stars also have the potential to evolve their own life, on their own planets, over a staggeringly long length of time. Just think of the incredible civilizations that haven't yet come into existence, destined to grow up in a much older and emptier universe.

What will they think of the future cosmos? They certainly won't know that our universe originated with a Big Bang, since all the leftover light and radiation will fade until it's invisible in just two trillion years, effectively deleting all the evidence we have the privilege of observing now. Those distant life forms might just declare that their galaxy was the only thing in the entire universe; they wouldn't know about any of the others. All the other galaxies would have drifted away.

When stars die, massive gas clouds are all that remain. Those clouds are usually the birthplaces of new stars, which engage in a sort of star cannibalism. New stars consume and burn the dead remnants of other stars, but the recycling process isn't 100% efficient. Stars lose hydrogen and heat all the time through their powerful stellar winds and radiation.

Eventually, there won't be enough raw materials left for new stars to form, and the very last star in the universe will fade away. The universe's review rating will go from one star to none. If anyone's around to witness that, it'll be a very sad day indeed.

Without the abundance of energy that stars provide, any surviving life will have to face the hard truth: it will be futile to try and survive longer. Life is a very organized system living in a universe that's always tending toward disorder. The point is, nobody's going to live forever; the law of entropy makes it so.

But life is pretty foolhardy in that sense. We've seen it in ourselves; we'll survive at all costs. All life will end one day, but the death of the last star probably won't be the death of life quite yet. We'll just have to see how far we can persist.

❖ TURNING OFF THE LIGHTS

In the aftermath of every star's death lies a stellar remnant. Every red dwarf and sun-like star will eventually fade away into a white dwarf star. Larger stars go out with a bang and collapse into ultra-dense neutron stars, spinning hundreds of times per second. The most massive stars blow up intensely, then meet their fate as black holes.

With no light left to give, and no fusion left to burn, our universe will be running out of free energy sources. With everything constantly blowing up, falling apart, and tending to a more disordered state, hydrogen clouds will get spread out to nothingness, ruining the chances of new stars forming. The atoms of our planet, our society, and your own body will become spread across the Milky Way over quadrillions of years, forming a tiny part of what little remained of our decaying galaxy.

The very last lights in the universe will be white dwarf stars. Despite being dead, they're the most stable light sources in the universe. Their shine comes from leftover heat rather than a fusion reaction, so they're more like a hot ember than a burning fire. Their only method of cooling down is to emit light.

As they cool from an impressive temperature of 40,000°C, they could keep our cosmos illuminated for up to a quadrillion (1,000,000,000,000,000) years. Eventually, our distant descendants may relax in the wasted heat of dead stellar corpses, long after every solar system in the universe has been destroyed.

White dwarf stars will eventually cool off as well, fading into a deep crimson red before cooling off entirely. After a quintillion (1,000,000,000,000,000,000) years have passed, absolutely no light will be left, and we'll be cast adrift in a perfectly dark universe. White dwarf stars will eventually turn into frozen black dwarf stars. That's the end of the road for all stars. We certainly don't have a bright future.

❖ PROTONS FALL APART

Not surprisingly, even after every star has frozen into a dead rock, our universe will still be capable of causing more chaos and destruction.

Some theories predict that protons, one of the basic pieces of atoms themselves, might start to decay and fall apart after an unimaginable length of time. After around 10^{33} (1,000,000,000,000,000,000,000,000,000,000,000) years have elapsed, ordinary matter might begin to disintegrate as its protons decayed and disappeared.

If humanity were somehow still living in the cosmos during this far-flung age, we would inevitably have to deal with the unpleasant problem of our bodies slowly dissolving into elementary particles. If protons do end up decaying, everything in the universe will disintegrate, ending any surviving planets, stellar remnants, asteroids, and strains of life. If this is what finally gets us, at least it will look epic.

Fortunately, proton decay is still totally theoretical, and depending on how the theory evolves, it might turn out to be completely wrong. Unfortunately, the matter of our survival doesn't really depend on proton decay, since we're basically doomed either way. Regardless of what happens in the distant future, black holes will dominate an empty void of a few faint photons and basic particles.

❖ BLACK HOLES VANISH

Black holes suck. You'd need to travel faster than light to get out of a black hole, and that's why nothing ever leaves. It was therefore a pretty big shock in 1974 when Stephen Hawking discovered that black holes must be leaking tiny amounts of energy into space and evaporating away.

Empty space itself is actually a dynamic place filled with trillions of particles and antiparticles always bursting into existence, chilling for a fraction of a second, and then going back to their matter-antimatter couples and annihilating each other. When these little particles suddenly appear, they borrow a tiny amount of energy from empty space, exist as solid particles briefly, then immediately give their borrowed energy back as they disappear. In this endless cycle, everything is balanced.

Black holes are capable of destroying that balance, leading to their own downfall. When a particle-antiparticle pair suddenly pops into existence right above the black hole's event horizon—the point of no return—one of the two particles might fall into the black hole, leaving the other particle alone and abandoned. That particle, no longer doomed to be annihilated by its couple, can now escape. Since the other particle is gone, the black hole has literally created a particle from nothing. That can't happen, so the leftover particle carries away a tiny amount of energy from the black hole as compensation.

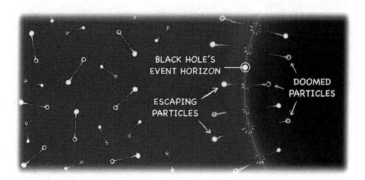

This process isn't a paradox; it's just a very complicated way of robbing a black hole of mass. Every particle that bursts into existence around a black hole steals a tiny bit of its mass and energy, and after trickling away at an absurdly slow rate, even the monstrous black holes will eventually disappear forever. The smallest things in existence, subatomic particles, are capable of destroy-ing the largest objects in the universe, black holes. Over stupendously long spans of time, one by one, these tiny particles will steal mass from black holes, trickling away a tiny amount of energy known as *Hawking Radiation*.

The very smallest black holes will take 10^{67} years to vanish—already ten billion trillion trillion trillion tril-lion times longer than the current age of the universe. The largest black holes, especially the ones lurking in the cores of huge galaxies, could last for a thousand trillion trillion trillion times longer: a staggering 10^{106} years, the longest and most brutal waiting game in the universe.

When black holes finally wither away, they'll each explode spectacularly with a brilliant burst of gamma rays as bright as a supernova. There won't be anyone to witness those explosions in the far-flung universe, but at least the deadly black hole fireworks will look pretty.

After all the black holes have disintegrated into a bland and featureless bath of heat, our universe will fall into its final state, known as *Heat Death*. It won't really be hot at the end of the universe, but everything will have been turned into wasted heat, which is just a balmy collection of subatomic particles and low-energy rays of light.

Heat is the endpoint of everything, since it just sits around and disperses; nothing else happens once heat is the only thing that's left.

If the last black hole's evaporation is the effective expiry date of our universe, we get a cosmic shelf life of 10^{106} years. That's more years than there are atoms in the universe. In that enormous era, our little blip of existence is just a sliver of time. The entire starlit era of the universe—the era in which we have heat and light, lush planets, liquid water, an abundance of energy, and a chance for life to exist—accounts for only 0.00000000 00000000000000000000000000000000000000000000000 00000000000000000000000000000000000000001% of our universe's entire lifespan.

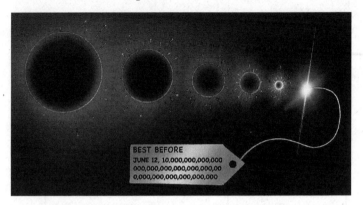

These early years are the universe's golden age. The universe won't ever be as pristine as it is right now. Every time we burn fuel and release its exhaust, every time we power city lights with electricity, and even every time we eat food and metabolize its energy, we're putting organized energy into a more disorganized and messy state, moving our entire universe closer to its ultimate fate. Every breath you take is creating more chaos and disorder.

But don't worry too much. There are burning stars and swirling galaxies out there. Those things are making far worse of a mess in our universe than we ever will.

❖ EVERYTHING TURNS TO IRON

If protons are still in one piece and nothing dramatic happens in the future, it's possible that little bits of matter could survive. Those include the remains of planets, the frozen cores of dead stars, and even atoms that once were a part of humanity. The problem is that these atoms would slowly undergo a weird sort of quantum activity known as cold fusion, in which atoms slowly bloop together and apart. Heavier atoms split into lighter ones, while lighter atoms gradually merge into heavier ones.

While we generally think of nuclear fusion as something that only happens in the burning hot cores of massive stars, it could still happen in the frozen future of a dead universe, just over quintillions of years. Cold fusion doesn't make logical sense, but then again, very few things caused by quantum effects actually make sense.

Iron is the most stable element in the universe. Tiny atoms like carbon or oxygen would be fused into iron, while massive elements like uranium and gold would be broken apart into iron. Over the unimaginable length of around 10^{1500} years, any surviving matter might clump together into cold spheres of iron known as *iron stars*. The amount of time it would take for these to exist is not even worth attempting to wrap your head around, although it's a great thought to keep you up at night.

BEYOND THE END

Even if planets get cooked, stars burn out, matter disintegrates, black holes evaporate, and iron stars freeze forever, space itself will still exist. In fact, as long as dark energy keeps pushing our universe steadily apart and space gets colder, darker and larger, it will continue to exist *forever*.

Across an infinite span of time, the awesome and terrifying possibilities for the future of the universe are endless. No amount of brainpower, gallons of coffee, or lying awake at three in the morning can help the human brain grasp the idea of infinite time. If our universe could exist forever, our story is far from over, even after our cosmos is totally dead.

❖ QUANTUM FLUCTUATIONS

Empty space is filled with quantum fluctuations of particles and antiparticles randomly popping into existence and disappearing. Conveniently, they don't fade away or slow down in the future; they just keep going on and on forever, filling empty space with the occasional flicker. Since quantum fluctuations are random, there's no certainty as to where particles could suddenly appear. In the empty vacuum of space, an atom could spontaneously form if the correct particles just appeared in the right place at the right time. With enough time and luck, perhaps a complete molecule of atoms could suddenly erupt into existence. If multiple molecules coincidentally appeared in close proximity, we could even make complex structures, all scattered across billions of light-years in a dead universe.

Coincidences are rare, but with enough waiting and being in the right place at the right time, random flukes are bound to happen eventually. For example, at some point within the unfathomable timespan of $10^{10^{50}}$ years, a basketball should suddenly appear in the middle of a perfect empty void. While this process would take one trillion trillion trillion trillion orders of magnitude longer than the entire lifespan of our universe, it *isn't* forever—and because it isn't forever, it *will* happen eventually.

When you think hard enough about it, maybe that's how our universe was born.

❖ A UNIVERSE FROM NOTHING

We can theorize all we want about what happened just after the birth of our universe, but we're at a loss to imagine what could've happened before it. If the universe is, by definition, the totality of everything in existence, where did it come from?

Near the end of the nineteenth century, the emerging field of thermodynamics had a very perplexing question: why is our universe not *already* dead, given that it has probably existed for an infinite amount of time before we came along? After an infinite amount of time, there should be nothing left. Planets, stars, and galaxies should have disintegrated into nothingness if they ever existed.

The physicist Ludwig Boltzmann theorized that perhaps our universe was just a quantum fluctuation within a much older and emptier dead universe—a universe that might have once harboured other stars, galaxies, and perhaps even life, but is now extinct.

We would have no way of knowing about their existence, let alone delving into their history books.

They certainly couldn't have known that humanity would ever exist in their distant future; they would have no idea that our universe would exist a long time after their universe had died—the ultimate cliffhanger.

A fundamental rule in our universe is that nothing can come from nothing. How could our universe, which is filled with matter and energy, have originated from a quantum fluctuation of purely empty space?

A theory in cosmology, known as the *zero-energy universe hypothesis*, predicts that all the positive energy of matter in our universe is exactly equal to all the negative energy of gravity, that there are an equal number of up-spinning particles as there are down-spinning particles, that every wave of light has equally many positive crests and negative troughs, and that all the matter in the universe is coupled with an equal and opposite amount of antimatter. When you add it all together, our universe would be a perfect zero—a universe originated from nothingness.

❖ WHOLE NEW UNIVERSES

There's an effect in statistical mechanics known as the *Poincaré recurrence theorem*, and while it certainly doesn't find itself in the spotlight of textbooks, it makes a freaky and awesome prediction for the future of our universe.

The recurrence theorem was first proposed by Henri Poincaré in 1890. It states that if you take a set of objects, shake them around, and let them randomly scatter and bounce, every object will eventually and randomly fall right back into its original starting position, resetting the cycle from the start.

As an example, imagine the recurrence theorem happening in a giant ball pit. If you put three balls in a ball pit, shake them around, and let them bounce for several minutes, the balls might end up back where they started after several minutes. If you put ten balls in the ball pit, it might take several years for them to randomly bounce back to their original starting positions.

The observable universe, on the other hand, contains around a billion trillion trillion trillion trillion trillion subatomic particles bouncing around, and while it would take an absurd amount of time, an analysis by physicists Sean Carroll and Jennifer Chen predicted that our universe *could* eventually repeat itself.

Ever hear people say YOLO (you only live once)? Well, our current model of cosmology, the process of quantum fluctuations, and the nature of infinity leads us to a very different conclusion.

If you put this book down right now, sat there, and waited for ten billion trillion trillion trillion trillion (10^{56}) orders of magnitude longer than the entire lifespan of the universe, the odds are pretty good that you'd be able to watch a new universe randomly explode, settle down, and randomly come together to make an *identical* copy of this current universe.

In the absurdly distant future, the most bizarre coincidence could happen: all the particles in the cosmos randomly end up in the exact same positions they're in today. That means there'd be an exact copy of you, sitting exactly where you're sitting right now, and reading this exact book. They'd be thinking about the future copy of themself that'd exist in *their* distant future. They'd have absolutely no clue that *you* ever existed in *their* distant past.

If you want to see the unimaginably distant future, simply take a look around you. For all you know, you might already be there.

❖ SOMETIME IN FOREVER

Our universe will exist for a huge amount of time after we're gone. The era of life is fleeting in the big picture compared to the lifespans of planets, let alone black holes, let alone the possible iron stars. But the atoms that make up our bodies today could potentially survive all the way out to those far-flung ages—and perhaps even beyond them.

If our world is consumed by the dying Sun, and if our material happens to sink into the Sun's core, then our individual atoms will find themselves stuck inside a white dwarf, turned black dwarf, eventually turned iron star.

While we won't get to see those distant times ourselves, at least a tiny part of us will be there.

No matter how long we try to survive, our universe has an unbreakable law in place that blatantly states we can't exist forever. Entropy will eventually get the better of us, whether we like it or not.

Despite the incredible thoughts our brains are capable of stirring up, there will be a last conscious experience at some point—which is as saddening as it is uplifting. With a finite amount of time, we have originality, which is truly everything humanity stands for. We are currently living in that tiny fraction of the universe's existence where life is possible. And even if this era is a tiny part of the whole story of the cosmos, it's still absurdly long by our human standards. We, in the coming trillions of years, will have the opportunity to explore a massive swath of the universe before entropy finally forces us into nonexistence.

Or perhaps it's simply better not to think about these things.

PART 5

LIFE OUT THERE

WHO WE REALLY ARE IN THE COSMOS

Let's take a moment to reflect. Who exactly *are* you?

You're a collection of cells working together. You only exist at this point in the Earth's history because the arrangement of cells *you* have are better at surviving and reproducing than most of the 5,000,000,000 to 50,000,000,000 other species that have gone extinct over the Earth's entire history. As mentioned in the 1997 book *The Biology of Rarity*, over 99% of all the species that have ever existed are now extinct. Yet here you are.

You're also a collection of tiny particles that have been through a *lot* in their backstory: they burst into existence after space itself collapsed at the birth of our universe; they joined together to form atoms; they smashed together into heavier atoms in the cores of giant exploding stars; they cycled through millions of plants and animals over Earth's history, and now, against the longest odds ever, some seven octillion (7,000,000,000,000,000,000,000,000,000) random atoms are joined together in your body today.

Those particles aren't just sitting there doing nothing. They're reading this book, and they're thinking about the universe that they came from. How is that possible? Why are you able to ponder that question in the first place? Take another moment to realize that you, in the very act of reading this book, are making a bunch of dead particles think about themselves. From a cosmic point of view, you are pretty awesome.

Life is one of the strangest concepts in the universe. But we've invented a very artificial definition of life. When we think about life, we might be thinking about getting an education, getting a job, earning enough money, raising a family, making sure we have food and water, making sure we have a place to live, and so on.

When people say "that's just life," they're almost always talking about life in the context of human society. Like most of the definitions humans have created, it doesn't really take the whole truth into account.

THE INNER WORKINGS OF LIFE

When you look at how a living thing works, it's like a fractal of hundreds of little pieces working together—and each of those pieces usually contains hundreds of smaller pieces working together.

An anatomist is someone who studies the human body, but anatomy is just a fancy version of biology, which is just a fancy version of chemistry, which is really just a fancy version of particle physics—and therefore, every anatomist is really just a highly-exalted particle physicist. Let's take this from the bottom up.

❖ PARTICLE PHYSICS

Your most basic pieces are subatomic particles. They are totally mindless; they don't do anything except exist. In fact, every particle in your body is so simple that we can define everything about them with just three numbers: a specific amount of mass, a specific amount of electric charge, and a spin. That's it.

All of the wildly complex events in the universe—the burning fusion in the stars, the photosynthesis in the green leaves, and even the thoughts going through your mind—are based on nothing more than these basic particles interacting with each other. None of the particles are complicated—there are just so many of them. In your own body, you've got several hundred octillion of them.

Life begins with two tiny particles called *up-quarks* and *down-quarks*. They are absurdly tiny; for a size reference, a quark compared to your body is like your body compared to the Milky Way galaxy.

Up-quarks and down-quarks have only a few properties: down-quarks have a slight negative charge, and up-quarks have a slight positive charge. Both of them have a little bit of mass. That's about it.

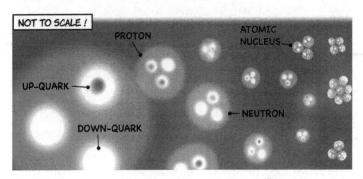

Particles don't really behave like solid balls. They don't look like anything, since the very act of "seeing" something requires us to shine light onto it, and most waves of light are *larger* than the particles themselves, so we can't directly see them.

Particles behave like abstract, fuzzy, and blurry force fields. Thanks to a wacky quantum effect known as the wave function, your particles could exist anywhere, from within your body to the outer edge of the universe. In fact, they exist in millions of places at the same time.

Since it's all random, when we average out all the possible locations that all the particles in your body could possibly be, we end up with an approximate collection of mass and charge that is, more or less, shaped like you.

Both up-quarks and down-quarks are never by themselves. Quarks usually bind together in groups of three. When two up-quarks and one down-quark bind together, we get a positively charged group of three: a proton. When two down-quarks and one up-quark bind together, their charges exactly balance each other out, and we get an uncharged group of three: a neutron.

As anyone who's played with magnets knows, you need to push really hard to get two of the same charges together. Some particles tend to repel each other violently. Your entire body would instantly explode and dissolve into subatomic particles if it weren't for two other elusive particles binding them all together: *gluons* and *mesons*.

Gluons are weird objects that don't really exist as a solid particle, but rather pop in and out of existence, everywhere, all at once, all the time. When nothing is in their way, they quickly vanish without a trace, but when they're around repulsive quarks, they interact with such a massive pull that they force the quarks together. It's like a group hug between three people, two of whom just hate each other and one of whom loves everyone. Thanks to gluons, our protons and neutrons don't explode.

In the atomic nucleus, protons and neutrons are packed tightly. Just like before, we've got a bunch of positively charged things that are trying to blast themselves away from each other. The nucleus would explode, if it weren't for the other weird particle called a meson. Mesons suddenly appear and interact with the protons, binding them together with over a hundred times more force than their feeble repulsion. It's thanks to them that your body doesn't instantly explode.

❖ ATOMS AND CHEMISTRY

Every atom in the universe is swarmed with electrons— tiny negatively charged particles that make our atoms magnetically charged. While old-school atom diagrams make electrons look like solid balls that orbit around in circles, the truth is that electrons behave like wacky quantum waves, existing in a cloud of many possible places at the same time. An electron forms a sort of blurry fuzz of negative charge.

When an atom has lots of electrons, they produce force fields of negativity around the atom, called *electron orbitals*. These orbitals are basically layers of blurry electrons. The innermost layer can hold two electrons, the second layer can hold eight, the third layer can hold eighteen, and so on.

Atoms are tiny packets full of energy. Once again, a basic rule of this universe is that objects always tend toward their lowest, most stable energy state. Atoms can get to that stable state by filling up their electron layers. That means they've got to fill their first layer with two electrons, their second layer with eight electrons, and so on.

Some atoms, like helium and neon, already have their outer layer totally filled up with electrons, so they quietly drift around and don't interact with other atoms very much. But when atoms have free spots in their electron layers, they have to look elsewhere, and that's when chemistry happens.

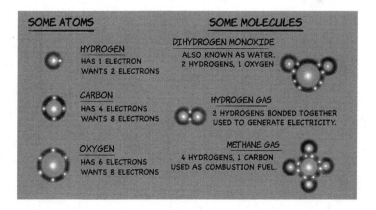

SOME ATOMS

HYDROGEN
HAS 1 ELECTRON
WANTS 2 ELECTRONS

CARBON
HAS 4 ELECTRONS
WANTS 8 ELECTRONS

OXYGEN
HAS 6 ELECTRONS
WANTS 8 ELECTRONS

SOME MOLECULES

DIHYDROGEN MONOXIDE
ALSO KNOWN AS WATER.
2 HYDROGENS, 1 OXYGEN

HYDROGEN GAS
2 HYDROGENS BONDED TOGETHER
USED TO GENERATE ELECTRICITY.

METHANE GAS
4 HYDROGENS, 1 CARBON
USED AS COMBUSTION FUEL.

In order to totally fill their outer electron layers and reach their most stable state, atoms often do *covalent bonding*. This happens when an atom basically merges its outer electron layer with another atom. If two atoms merge their electron layers, those electrons keep going in a blurry quantum cloud of many locations at once—except now, they're free to exist in both atoms at the same time!

That means both atoms get bonus electrons, even if the electrons don't belong to them. If each of the merged atoms gets a full outer layer of electrons thanks to this weird quantum effect, they'll tend to stick together and make a couple, since both of them have settled in their most stable states. Sometimes it takes three atoms, or four, or many more. A huge molecule known as buckminster-fullerene consists of 60 carbon atoms bonded this way.

The main force holding you together is just a result of your atoms trying to fall into their most stable state. Laziness is a universal trait, exhibited even in our very atoms.

With a large palette of elements, we can create an estimated sixteen million different types of organic molecules, like chocolate, hand sanitizer, car fuel, water—and every amino acid in your body. All of them are held together just because each atom is sharing blurry clouds of electrons, reaching their lowest and most stable positions.

It's at this level that we can see two fundamental building blocks to life as we know it: carbon and water.

❖ FANTASTIC CARBON AND WATER

Saying that "carbon is important to life as we know it" is an understatement.

Out of all the atoms in your body, 1/5 of them are carbon. It forms the core of every amino acid in all your proteins, every nucleotide base in all of your DNA, every crevice of all your delicate cell membranes, and every microscopic molecule that cranks away inside your cells every single second.

The reason carbon is so effective at doing all this is because it needs four electrons to fill its outer layer, which means it can bond with up to four other atoms—the most out of any element in your body. Lame hydrogen can only make one bond. Oxygen can make chains at best with two bonds. Nitrogen can technically build flat sheets with its three bonds. Awesome carbon, however, can build complex three-dimensional structures with four bonds.

As well, carbon doesn't make crystals at normal temperatures and pressures, allowing it to slosh and mingle with all sorts of molecules in dynamic and fluid chemistry.

The other essential component of life on Earth is, of course, water.

The reason water is so amazing is because it is an expert at dissolving things. The two hydrogen atoms in a water molecule make a positively charged aura around them, while the single oxygen atom makes a shroud of negativity. That means water behaves like a magnet, so it sticks to itself. Better yet, it can stick to other solid objects and pull apart their bonds, basically dissolving just about anything.

Because of this, water is known as the *universal solvent*; it can easily dissolve dozens of salts, hundreds of sugars, and countless organic hydrocarbons—more materials than any other known liquid in the universe.

Carbon forms the core of complex molecular structures, and water provides it with a sloshy mixture to flow in. Combined with dozens of other molecules, these two miracle-makers of life are capable of producing amazing things.

❖ CELL BIOLOGY

Using nothing but particle charges and a law that makes all atoms tend toward their most stable positions, we can make the legendary double-helix ladder of life itself: DNA, with a twist—quite literally. DNA is a fascinating molecule, but as we know, it really can't do anything on its own. That's where the other proteins and enzymes floating around a cell come in handy.

When a cell begins to divide, a molecule known as the *helicase* is pulled onto the DNA, firing off a chemical reaction where the helicase starts snapping the hydrogen bonds holding the two strands of DNA together, essentially working like a zipper running down a chain, separating the double helix into two individual strands.

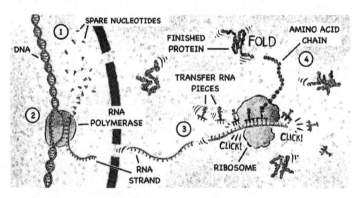

While this is happening, molecules known as *DNA polymerases* bond to the unzipped strands. Their magnetic charges pull in spare nucleotides that bind with each unzipped strand, which stitches together two new DNA strands, like an anti-zipper building two new chains out of each unzipped half of the chain. If we ever figured out how to do this with *real* zippers, it'd be amazing.

The micro-zippers aren't just effective; they're fast! DNA polymerases do their work at a feverish pace of around fifty nucleotides per second. That's equivalent to typing this entire book in an hour, easily putting even the most prolific authors to shame.

Our cells need to copy their DNA in order to divide and survive, but DNA is also essential for making the tiny machines that perform tasks around the cell, including the enzymes that copy DNA in the first place.

To do that task, massive molecules known as *RNA polymerases* attach to strands of DNA and start unzipping it, pulling in spare nucleotides and stitching together a little strand of RNA packed full of the information that codes for a certain protein to be built.

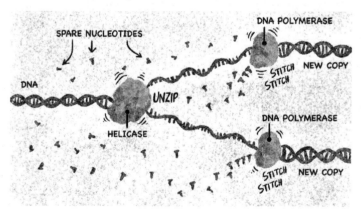

That package of RNA then randomly drifts throughout the watery interior of the cell, where another giant molecule, called a *ribosome*, bonds to it. Since certain atoms on the strand of RNA are magnetically charged, they pull on certain amino acids drifting around the cell and start snapping them together into a chain.

More nucleotides are magnetically drawn to the strand as it gets pulled through the ribosome, squeezing out a long string of amino acids. The shortest protein we know about is the *TAL protein*, found in fruit flies, which is eleven amino acids long. The longest one is *Titin protein*, found in our skeletal muscles, whose chain is a whopping 35,000 amino acids long. Incredibly, the whole process is so fast that a ribosome could whisk up a Titin protein in just 30 minutes.

Eventually, the strand of RNA hits an endpoint. On each strand, there's a specific set of molecules which cause the ribosome to cut off the chain, like a printer slicing a sheet of paper in half. The chain then gets released into the cell, and since amino acids are also magnetically charged, the whole chain suddenly folds up on itself and becomes a tightly-knit protein.

Thanks to the way that the amino acids are folded, each protein is best suited for a certain task. Some have bond snippers that can cut molecule chains, like *fidgetin*. Some bind well to viruses and serve as red flags, like *antibodies*. Some have moveable legs that can literally walk on tiny fibers, hauling bags of molecules around the cell, like *kinesin*.

But you won't have much luck making a protein do anything without a source of energy to power it. That's where the tiny molecular batteries come in.

❖ A SOURCE OF ENERGY

Adenosine triphosphate, or *ATP*, is like a little firecracker. It's a simple molecule made of a type of sugar known as adenosine, with three phosphate molecules bonded on its side. If the phosphate molecule on the end gets snapped off, it releases a massive amount of chemical energy—enough to power a cell's operations.

These little ATP batteries get pieced together inside the mitochondria—the power plants of the cell, as *everyone* says—and that involves a whole other reaction in which glucose sugars are broken down into smaller molecules, passed through a giant molecule known as an ATP synthase, and bonded to new phosphate firecrackers floating in the cell.

It usually takes several ATP batteries to charge up the molecules of a protein so that it can perform its task, and millions of proteins are operating inside each of your cells—every single second. According to the *National Library of Medicine*, the cells in our bodies burn through around 75 kilograms of ATP batteries every single day, which is possibly more than your entire body weight. In that sense, your body is like an empty power plant that constantly inhales air and consumes food to produce its fuel.

Every single day, you burn through the weight of a whole *person* in ATP alone!

❖ THE MEANING OF LIFE

What? You thought we'd have a whole chapter on life without talking about the meaning of it all?

Well, good news! From a scientific standpoint, there is no meaning of life. We've seen that your entire body is based on subatomic particles that are moving around randomly. If you don't think that particles moving around randomly has a meaning, then neither does life.

It's not as if molecules can "choose" to bond with things or "decide" to move to certain places, and yet the whole system still works. Life is a random and messy chemical reaction in which nothing is planned, but since there are so many tiny bits and pieces moving around, enough of them get to the right places.

Even as you read this sentence, tiny floodgates in your brain's neurons are opening up to let charged ions rush inside the cells. Once enough electric charge builds up inside a neuron, it zaps outward to other neurons and flashes across the brain. Nothing in that process ever "chooses" to send the signal. Everything is random. But somehow, that random zap of electricity is creating an actual experience in your mind. You're actually experiencing something as you read this. And this. And this too! It's not just a random chemical reaction. Or is it?

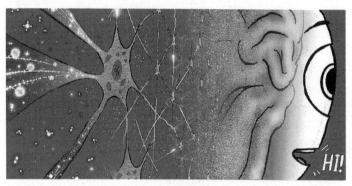

You can think about things and make decisions, even though everything in your brain is just a network of cells zapping each other, all of which are just molecules bouncing off each other, all of which are just atoms bonding to each other, all of which are just little particles behaving under the laws of physics.

So, what makes something alive? How is a living thing different from the dead stuff that makes up the rest of the universe?

❖ A SET OF INFORMATION

Even if life doesn't really have a meaning, life definitely acts with a sense of purpose.

A living cell is basically a tiny bubble of chemistry that doesn't tend to follow the rule of entropy—the law that makes everything fall apart into chaos. While a cell makes the environment around it more messy by eating and releasing material, it keeps itself in pristine condition, ordered, and tidy for a long time. It keeps itself together for a lot longer than normal dead chemistry would.

So perhaps that's what life is. Maybe life is a collection of dead stuff that uses energy to keep itself organized and prevent itself from falling into bits.

The other obvious goal of life is to reproduce.

We exist in this moment because 15,000 generations of humans decided to reproduce and have babies before us, all of whom eventually led to our existence today. Like we saw earlier, the game of life is an endless struggle for information to try and survive. The genetic code is everything.

The DNA in your body won't live forever because *you* won't live forever. But if you have a baby, your DNA can take its information and copy it into another living thing that will live longer than you. In an ideal world, the cycle of reproduction is an endless loop. Even though the individual strands of DNA are born and then die, the *information* in the DNA gets copied and pasted into the future, again and again, and quite literally tries to live forever.

Well then, is life just a foolhardy set of information that tries to cheat death by copying itself? Is the concept of "you" just the information that's coded in the specific order of the rungs of your DNA? Is all the other stuff— the water in your cells, the calcium in your bones, and the tissue in your muscles—just bonus equipment that your DNA evolved to keep itself safe, protected, and more capable of copying itself?

From the perspective of evolution, yes.

That means you are a clump of DNA that weighs just over 19 grams, and the rest of you is the mechanism that keeps those 19 grams of DNA safe, in the evolutionary hopes that you might eventually take it and copy it into an offspring. No pressure, of course.

So, what counts as life, then? If life is just a set of information that can copy itself, there are some weird things that technically count as being "alive," even though they don't look alive.

We don't think of viruses as being alive because they can't reproduce on their own. They have to invade our cells and hack them to make more copies of themselves. They're just big dead molecules that have a tiny bit of genetic code inside.

But over the history of the Earth, our cells have built up defences to stop viruses, and those viruses have evolved to match that. Only the viruses that randomly had tools to break through our cells' defences—and subsequently hack our cells—were able to reproduce, so only the more adapted types of viruses ended up surviving.

When you look at the virus that gives the common cold, the adenovirus, you can obviously see what it has evolved to help it sneak past our cells' defences: little rods to pick the locks of our cells' surfaces, and toxic proteins to rip apart our cell's lysosomes—those little bags of acid that usually dissolve viruses.

Are viruses alive? They're just little chunks of dead atoms. They are unable to move by themselves, so they just float around at random and interact with other molecules as they bump into them. But they literally evolved ways to copy and paste their set of genetic code into more of themselves. They are a set of information struggling to survive forever—not too different from us, really.

Even a crystal—something that's closer to a *rock* than a living cell—has a specific order and structure to its atoms. As more atoms fall onto the crystal, they bond according to the specific pattern of the crystal.

A salt crystal, for example, is made of atoms of chlorine and sodium that lock together in a cube shape. Their magnetic charges pull more sodium and chlorine atoms into the same cubic pattern. It's definitely a stretch, but a crystal is also a set of information that naturally makes copies of itself. Are crystals alive, then? Take it with a grain of salt, that's for sure.

❖ EMERGENCE

If there's one thing life is all about, it's an effect known as *emergence*. It's the fact that while really simple things can't do much by themselves, collectively they can do really complex things when functioning together. You can't build a city by yourself, for example. A million people, working alone, can't build a million cities. But a million people working on a shared city project can easily construct a huge and sprawling city in less than a decade.

Life works in the exact same way. A trillion individual atoms can't really hold any information, but in a cell, all of them work together in a system that can read DNA, build proteins, talk to other cells, and get tasks done. A trillion individual cells don't have any feelings, awareness, or thoughts, but they somehow do if you combine them together into a human brain.

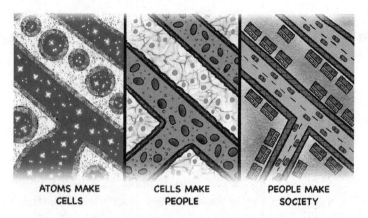

ATOMS MAKE
CELLS

CELLS MAKE
PEOPLE

PEOPLE MAKE
SOCIETY

When you think of social, political, technological and cultural movements throughout history, you realize that human society works in the same way. There are countless examples of effects, processes and phenomenon that all of humanity achieved together, but no one in the world attained by themself.

LIFE WHERE WE LEAST EXPECT IT

Okay. That last section probably didn't help us define precisely what life is. But it definitely demonstrates that "life" can be an amazingly wide range of things. As we keep looking for life beyond the Earth, we need to remember that not all life needs to look like Earth life.

To be honest, everyone is talking about the possibilities of life on the watery ice caps of Mars, deep in the oceans of Jupiter's moon Europa, and under the ice sheets of Saturn's moon Enceladus. Even as those worlds flaunt their water at us, there are new watery places being found across the solar system. In 2001, an underground ocean was discovered on Jupiter's moon Callisto, and in 2015, an underground ocean was found on Jupiter's largest moon Ganymede. In 2020, a research team found that even the asteroid Ceres likely has its own salty water under its rocky surface. In 2021, a study started looking for water on the moons of Uranus, and sure enough, *four* of them likely have water in them. The worlds of the cosmos are wetter than we thought.

We know how amazing water and carbon are; they're the stuff of life on Earth! When we search for life in space, we like to look for planets that orbit in the *habitable zone* around their stars. If a planet is too close to its star, it will toast and sizzle like a marshmallow. Too far away, and it will freeze. There's a specific zone, not too close and not too far from the star, where water can flow as a liquid. We're obsessed with it.

Humans evolved on a wet planet that has lots of carbon, and because of that, we're stuck with a bias toward the same sort of materials elsewhere in the universe.

Saturn's icy moon, Enceladus, was *so* suspected of having life that we dive-bombed the *Cassini* spacecraft into Saturn, plunging it to its doom in 2017, to prevent any chance of contaminating the moon's oceans.

People already say enough about the signs of life in the watery oceans of other planets, especially the ones that have a lot of carbon. That's our Earth bias kicking in and making us look for life as we know it.

But if we dare look for the unexpected, how big and wide are the possibilities for life as we don't know it? How many other types of life might be evolving into weird and wild organisms, across the cosmos, in places that we might totally overlook?

❖ LIFE IN THE SKIES

Near the end of 2020, there was a lot of hype around the upper atmosphere of Venus. Astronomers had found signs of *phosphine*, a molecule that's almost always produced by microbes here on Earth. Venus is truly the last place in the solar system you'd expect to find life. Its atmosphere is almost entirely made of carbon dioxide, crushed to 90 times the density of our Earth's atmosphere, cooked to a toasty 475°C, and soaked in corrosive sulphuric acid.

The lofty upper atmosphere of Venus actually has very mild pressures and temperatures, not unlike those you'd find on a summer afternoon here on Earth, but even the most hardy bacteria would shrivel up in the acid and the lack of water. But maybe Venusian microbes wouldn't be anything like the ones here on Earth.

Dr. Sara Seager and colleagues speculated in 2021 that perhaps microbes on Venus grow and thrive inside raindrops of sulphuric acid. Then, as the rain falls and vaporizes, they dry up and are lofted upward into the atmosphere as frazzled crisps where they can be caught by another droplet, soaked in the liquid, and begin their life cycle again. It's a circle of life based on the value of repeated agonizing vaporization. It sounds quite lovely.

The chances for life on Venus have been dwindling ever since volcanoes on Venus became a possible source of the phosphine gas. In fact, data from the SOFIA telescope showed that there might not have been any phosphine at all, but even so, the mystery is far from solved. Venus could have been filled with life back when it was thought to be habitable several billion years ago, and perhaps life has been struggling onward in the skies ever since the planet became a dead hellscape—living fossils of a once-lush planet.

If life can exist in the thin upper atmosphere of deadly Venus, that means the gas giant world of Jupiter is also a possible site for life as well. Hitting the headlines of *Nature Astronomy* in 2020 was the possibility of a cloud of water vapour covering Jupiter's thin upper atmosphere.

Jupiter's atmosphere is intense, to say the least. Subject to hurricanes larger than the entire Earth and zapped with lightning bolts as long as all of Australia, the skies of Jupiter could be the site of fantastic chemistry—even life. Living creatures could be rifting through the high clouds, surfing on the powerful winds that would keep them in the air against Jupiter's strong gravity.

It's not just Jupiter that is now drawing attention; so are *brown dwarf stars*.

A brown dwarf star isn't really a star; it's a giant ball of hydrogen and helium, much larger than Jupiter, that didn't quite become a star. Most of them are hot enough to have complex weather and chemistry in their atmospheres—and perhaps they could even hold life.

A study of the brown dwarf WISE J085510.83–0714442.5 showed that it contained almost all of the basic ingredients for life cruising along in its atmosphere, which is mostly made of hydrogen, but contains oxygen and nitrogen, as well as a jackpot of carbon. Now, admittedly, that's a bias toward Earth life again.

The deep layers of its atmosphere would crush and cook life as we know it, and the upper layers would be far too thin for anything to survive, but there's a sweet spot in the middle: a region where the atmosphere is a pleasant room temperature. If any creatures evolved in the clouds of a gas giant, they would be as light as the air itself, practically swimming through it like we swim through water.

❖ TRAPPED AND ADRIFT

Given how often we keep finding oceans under the surfaces of planets and moons in our solar system, it's very likely that many of the planets and moons elsewhere in the universe have underground oceans too. And since those oceans would be shielded from meteorite impacts and radiation by a huge layer of rock, they could serve as extremely safe habitats.

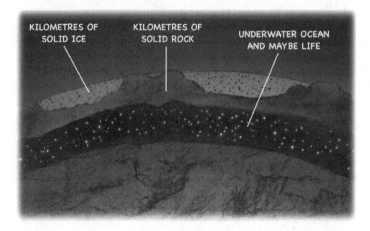

KILOMETRES OF SOLID ICE

KILOMETRES OF SOLID ROCK

UNDERWATER OCEAN AND MAYBE LIFE

In fact, with so many planets possibly having water under their surfaces, we might be able to expand the idea of a "habitable planet" to worlds that have no suns at all: rogue planets.

A lonely new planet was discovered in 2012, and it challenged our ideas on how planets come to exist in the first place. It wasn't in the tranquil warmth of its sun, but rather in the cold void of interstellar space. It seems that the planet was bitterly rejected by the star it formed around. Perhaps it had the same kind of sibling rivalry that the Earth had in the early solar system.

CFBDSIR 2149-0403, as the forsaken world was named, was the first rogue planet ever discovered, and it was the first of many. By the end of 2021, nearly 200 rogue planets had been spotted across the galaxy.

Most planets end up as rogues by getting slingshotted out of their solar systems, since the birth of a solar system isn't always pretty. The number of planets that meet their fate this way is staggering: a 2012 study at the Kavli Institute estimated that there could be up to 20 quadrillion (20,000,000,000,000,000) rogue planets in our galaxy alone. That's 100,000 rogue planets for every one regular sunny planet.

Most people assumed these planets would be nothing more than cold, dead husks. Nobody imagined that anything could be living on a planet that had cooled to −270°C, that's for sure! Here's the catch: large planets usually have molten cores, which slowly leak energy outward toward the surface. Any moons that orbit the planet would stretch and squeeze it like clay, slowly warming it up.

If a rogue planet had an underground ocean with hot mineral jets shooting up from the warm mantle, then some kind of ecosystem could survive. The spaces for life would be pretty limited, but life would have a huge span of time to develop; the thick layer of ice, covering the entire underground ocean, would act like a colossal shield and protect against asteroid impacts. Underneath the ocean, the planet's hot core would continue heating the planet for billions of years.

If intelligent life evolved, they might not ever find anything beyond their little layer of ocean. They might never know that there was ever a spectacular universe right above their little crust of ice.

LIFE WITHOUT THE ESSENTIALS

We keep assuming that water and carbon are the two key ingredients for life. But what if they're not? Orbiting around Saturn, there's a moon which, at first glance, looks strikingly similar to the Earth. It has oceans and lakes, beaches and sand dunes, and a dense atmosphere with clouds that produce rain.

Titan, however, is awfully cold, with its average summertime temperature peaking at a frigid $-180^{\circ}C$. Water is as hard as rock on the surface, carbon dioxide is frozen solid, and nitrogen gas is almost cold enough to flow as a liquid. Methane and ethane, which are familiarly gases used for combustion on Earth, exist as a liquid on Titan. They flow across the surface and produce lakes and basins with roiling rivers. Titan is covered in whole oceans of methane, which slowly evaporate and then fall from the upper atmosphere as methane rain.

Titan's surface has almost zero phosphorous and oxygen, which are both key ingredients in building the fragile lipid membranes that protect our cells.

As far as we know, lipids are the best way to go for building cell membranes because half of the molecule repels water, the other half of them attracts water, and all the lipids are attracted to each other. This causes a long sheet of clingy lipids to come together and pull themselves into a closed bubble.

It's kind of hard to build something in water, however, when the water is frozen as hard as rock.

❖ NITROGEN CELLS

To create a cell in a methane ocean, we would need some sort of molecule that was attracted and repelled by methane instead of water. In 2015, researchers at Cornell University simulated little cells, which they called *azotosomes*, that were made of nitrogen and methane instead of phosphorous and carbon—and it worked at temperatures of −180°C instead of our usual Earthly temperature of 15°C.

The molecule that makes this possible, called acrylo-nitrile, is often used in textile factories here on Earth. It is deemed highly toxic as it's known to cause cancer.

On Titan, it might literally be the building block of life.

If nitrogen cells ever evolved in a vast ocean of methane, they'd breathe gases in the air, which would eventually have an effect on the atmosphere. Our own Earth went through a huge incident called the *Great Oxidization Event*, which occurred when cyanobacteria, living and breathing in our oceans, sucked most of the nitrogen and methane from our skies and replaced it with oxygen.

Interestingly, a 2010 study found that the air near Titan's surface has much less hydrogen than the air up high in the atmosphere. No one knows what—or who, for that matter—could be causing hydrogen to disappear like that.

For now, let's not waste our breath on this.

❖ SHADOW BIOSPHERE

On planets of all shapes and sizes, no matter what awful environment covers the surface, there's always a chance you'll find a familiar trace of liquid water. Titan's surface behaves really weirdly; while continents on Earth move a few inches each year, the land on Titan shifts by dozens of *kilometres*. It's like continental drift on steroids.

While Titan is definitely too cold for a hot molten mantle, astronomers are now almost certain that there's a massive underground ocean, kept warm by the powerful gravity of Saturn. Yeah, once again, we've found an ocean in the solar system.

If Titan really has an underground ocean of liquid water, topped by a crust with fresh oceans of liquid methane, we could hypothetically get *two* different types of life existing on the same world! One would live deep underground, based on ordinary water and carbon, and the other would live on the freezing surface, based on cold methane and ethane.

In 2010, the *Cassini* spacecraft's RADAR team found evidence of volcanoes on the surface of Titan spewing up liquid water from the underground ocean. To any methane-based life form, liquid water would be so hot that it would instantly kill them, just like molten magma would instantly kill us.

If intelligent life is dwelling on the surface of Titan, and if they're looking for life beyond Titan, they probably aren't looking for liquid water, just like we don't suspect life exists on molten lava planets. They'd be looking for methane, obviously. If they discovered *us*, our tendency to drink liquid water would be quite a shock, to say the least!

THE SCIENTISTS ON TITAN HAVE CONCLUDED
THAT THERE'S PROBABLY NO LIFE ON EARTH

ANALOGUE CHEMISTRY

If life could exist in an ocean that had no water, could we take this a step further and imagine life evolving without any organic chemistry in the first place? In other words, even though carbon, oxygen, and nitrogen seem really important to life as we know it, are they actually so special to life in general?

The bonding of some atoms can be very similar to the bonding of other atoms, producing substances that look and behave the same, even with completely different atoms. Hydrogen, fluorine, chlorine, bromine, and iodine, for example, can all bond with sodium. We're used to eating regular table salt, which is sodium chloride (NaCl). But you can also mix sodium with hydrogen (NaH), fluorine (NaF), bromine (NaBr), and iodine (NaI), because all those elements bond with sodium the same way that chlorine does. All of them look and feel just like sodium chloride, salt. They don't all taste as good, but that's not the point.

If we could build *life* out of these alternative atoms instead of the usual ones, would it still work in the same way? Would it count as being alive?

❖ SWIMMING IN SULPHUR

Water is critical to all life on Earth. It's great at dissolving other materials, which makes it a fantastic chemical soup base for almost everything. Water consists of oxygen atoms bonded to two hydrogen atoms (H_2O)—but sulphur can also bond with two hydrogens to make a colourless gas known as hydrogen sulphide (H_2S).

At the chilly temperature of −60°C, it condenses down into a yellowish liquid, behaving just like normal water. Could an exotic form of life thrive in a freezing ocean of hydrogen sulphide on some distant planet?

There are already types of cells right here on Earth, known as sulphate-reducing bacteria, that eat sulphur as their energy source instead of oxygen. They devour sulphate and release hydrogen sulphide—our doppelgänger of water. The sulphur they emit kicks oxygen out of the atmosphere.

These tiny bacteria could have been the culprits of the most catastrophic mass extinction in history: the Permian-Triassic Mass Extinction Event, which killed off 90% of all life 252 million years ago. A study in 2021 suggested that as the world's temperatures went up, these sulphur-eating bacteria thrived and vibed. Along with volcanic eruptions, and perhaps a meteorite impact, they could have killed off millions of species. Life that loves hydrogen sulphide might sound like it belongs on another planet, but it's possible that they've already been *here* on Earth.

❖ CELLS OF TOXIC ARSENIC

Phosphorous can join together with oxygen to form phosphate (PO_4). It holds together the rungs of our DNA ladder, keeping our genetic code from crumbling to bits. The proteins in our cells also need phosphate's energy in those little ATP batteries that are used to power our cells.

Interestingly, one of the most toxic elements in the world could hypothetically replace phosphorous in these systems. Arsenic is just awful, and when you join it together with oxygen, you get a really toxic version of phosphate: arsenate (AsO_4). But because it is also so similar, it could be a whole new building block of life.

Eating arsenate is a quick way to end up in the hospital or worse, resulting in lesions and cancer. But arsenate has a curious potential: it can bond in the same way that phosphate can. If you jam it between the rungs of our DNA ladder, it should be able to hold it together. It'd be a freaky sort of DNA impostor.

A mind-blowing strain of bacteria known as GFAJ-1 was discovered in 2010 by a research team led by Dr. Felisa Wolfe-Simon, and it changed everything we thought we knew about the chemistry of life… for about two years.

The bacteria seemed to have a superpower: they seemed to be able to take the phosphate in their cells and swap it out with deadly arsenate molecules. Not only that, they seemed to thrive.

Without any trace of phosphorous in GFAJ-1, people began to wonder if this was actually a species of bacteria that was based on arsenic instead of phosphorous. It hinted that our world might contain something called a *shadow biosphere*: maybe there's an entire ecosystem of arsenic impostors living among us, filled with arsenic microbes. Maybe they stayed far away from us because we contained phosphorous, which would be toxic to a creature that used arsenic.

The speculation was fun, but sadly, it all got proven wrong.

Two years after GFAJ-1 was found, experiments found an error in the original study. No arsenic was actually found in the innards of the bacteria, and it turned out that GFAJ-1 was just a regular bacterium with a devious resistance to the deadly effects of arsenic—which is still really cool, but a bit of a letdown.

Arsenate-based DNA was found to work a bit like soft tissue paper in water. It could hold together like regular DNA, but as soon as it was immersed in water, its arsenic bonds would almost instantly shatter, and the strand would dissolve in just a few seconds. So much for that idea.

❖ LIVING ROCKS OF SILICON

Let's look at carbon, the miracle-maker of life. It has four empty spaces in its outer electron layer, so it can make a bond with up to four other atoms at a time. Silicon is over twice as heavy as carbon, and it can also bond with up to four atoms. Just like carbon can form methane (CH_4), silicon can form silane (SiH_4), and just like carbon can form carbon dioxide (CO_2) when mixed with oxygen, silicon produces silicon dioxide (SiO_2) deep within sedimentary rocks. For almost any molecule that carbon can make, its doppelgänger silicon can make it too.

This really makes us wonder: why is every organism on this planet made of carbon-based materials without a trace of silicon?

Silicon is just as capable as carbon when it comes to bonding. But in terms of its reactions, it is kind of an introvert. When silicon mixes with oxygen gas, it turns into solid silica crystals like quartz. When we breathe out, we're essentially oxidizing the extra carbon in our bodies, which allows it to escape as a gas. Unfortunately, a silicon-based life form would exhale solid quartz rocks if they breathed in oxygen. That'd be pretty uncomfortable, to say the least.

In order for silicon-based life to thrive at normal temperatures, it would have to live on a planet with no oxygen in the atmosphere. Since it'd basically be made of solid rock, a silicon creature could get its energy by consuming solid crystals and then slowly digesting them over thousands of years. Given how long their life cycle would take, would we actually assume it was alive, or would we just call it a weird rock?

If we think silicon life is a lost cause just because it turns into solid rock, we might just be too biased. We live on a planet where the watery oceans are warm enough to be a liquid, but silicon rocks are solid. Of course liquids are better than solids if you're trying to brew life. So maybe we're just looking at the wrong temperature.

Think about the situation on Titan: methane flows as a liquid, but the water is frozen as hard as rock on the surface. If there were creatures on Titan, they'd be familiar with liquid methane, and they probably wouldn't assume that life could ever evolve in water. Of course, life probably couldn't evolve in a frozen hunk of ice, but as we know, that's the wrong idea: water can definitely harbour life, just at a higher temperature where it flows as a liquid.

Silicon crystals look dead and rocky on Earth, but they can get involved in really complex chemistry in a hot, molten condition. At temperatures above 1,710°C on a molten planet, silica crystals would melt into a flowing magma, and even silicon, which is pretty inert here on Earth, would become as energetic as the carbon chemistry in our oceans.

While carbon could be the main building block of life on watery planets, silicon could be the key ingredient to life on molten planets glowing at thousands of degrees. It's a hotly debated topic, that's for sure.

Perhaps the silicon-based life isn't out there, but right here on Earth. Remember that Titan might have an underground layer of liquid water *and* have oceans of liquid methane on its surface. If methane-based life could exist on the surface of Titan while water-based life coexists underground, then we could even imagine the same thing happening on Earth!

Our planet supports a surface layer of liquid water, and it also has an underground mantle of molten magma where the most common rock is silicon dioxide. Just imagine how shocking that would be to discover aliens not above us, but below us.

THE MOST EXOTIC LIFE

If life could exist on planets completely different from Earth, living in a liquid completely different from water, made from materials completely different from regular chemistry, how far could we go?

What are the wildest possibilities for life in the universe?

To answer this, let's decide where we finally draw the line between living and non-living things. At what point is something definitely alive or definitely dead? If we take a more practical definition of life—a creature that is made of cells, eats food, and has some sort of genetic code—then the possibilities for life in the universe probably end here.

But let's take NASA's vague definition of life: any self-sustaining chemical system capable of Darwinian evolution.

Based on that, "life" is just a set of information that is able to hold itself together, grab the material around it, and use that material to build copies of itself before it falls apart. If we get that abstract, there are possibilities for life that defy our imagination.

❖ PLASMA IN DEEP SPACE

When we think of life in space, we tend to think of creatures living on an *object* in space, not within the void of space itself.

A 2007 study in the *New Journal of Physics* looked at the baffling possibility of life chilling in the cold vacuum of space. More specifically, the study looked at sparse clouds of dust and plasma in the middle of space. It found, eerily, that cosmic clouds are more alive than we may think.

In the middle of interstellar space, there are huge clouds of hot dusty plasma that are made of a fine mixture of free-floating charged particles and larger pieces of dust. Our entire solar system is thought to have come from one of those clouds that collapsed under its gravity. But even before the collapse occurs, before a star is born, and before planets clump together, the clouds are teeming with activity.

Plasma is made of charged particles, so it's electrostatic as it moves. When the fine dust pieces drift through the plasma, they also become static and begin to attract and repel each other. In the study's computer simulation, scientists looked at how the dust moved through the cloud. In a freaky and beautiful way, lifeless magnetic dust flowed into the shape of a spiralling cylinder.

That structure was able to produce a copy of itself by dragging the dust around it. Two dusty spirals could drag on each other and change each others' shape, causing them to dissolve instantly if they were damaged, or reproduce more effectively if they became more sturdy. Does this count as life?

Dusty plasma in the middle of empty space could be making complex structures across the galaxy at this very moment, and since they could thrive in stellar dust clouds, the atmospheres of stars, and even the huge plasmic jets shooting out of galaxies, these spirals might literally be the most common species of life in the entire universe.

❖ LIFE ON A NEUTRON STAR

One of the most far-flung ideas for life in space probably came from the American astrophysicist Frank Drake, a pioneer in the field of radio astronomy and the search for life beyond the Earth. He suggested that it might be possible for life to form and evolve on the surfaces of *neutron stars*.

A neutron star is what you get when a massive star collapses on itself and blows up in a supernova. The core of the star gets crushed to such unimaginable density that protons and electrons are literally crushed together into neutrons. Some supernova explosions are so utterly powerful that they collapse themselves into black holes; other supernova explosions are slightly weaker, such that they collapse into a tiny spinning ball, precariously perched at some of the highest densities allowed by the laws of physics. Neutron stars are right on the brink of becoming black holes. Only the intense force of the neutrons pushing against each other stops that collapse.

The temperature there is often a balmy 100 million degrees Celsius. The gravity pulls you down 100 billion times stronger than it does on Earth. The whole star spins up to 700 times per second in extreme cases. It's so bafflingly dense that a single tablespoon of the surface weighs as much as Mount Everest. It's not your ideal summer vacation, to say the least.

It's the absolute last place you'd ever expect to find life.

However, as Frank Drake pointed out in an interview in 1973, the surfaces of neutron stars have a very diverse pallet of atomic material. You won't find regular chemistry on a neutron star, since the atoms are crushed to bits. Instead, you'll find subatomic particles sloshing around on the hot surface. Those particles could, in theory, join together to make long chains and clusters.

While molecules would be impossible, the particles might be able to smoosh together to make complex structures—maybe even life.

On a neutron star, Drake suggested that life could get its source of energy from nuclear fusion, which would be pretty easy to do in the ludicrous heat and pressure. This sort of "life" is hard to imagine for us earthlings, but the laws of physics haven't ruled it out.

If nuclear life ever existed on the surface of a neutron star, it would function with a life cycle that'd be billions of times faster than ours. Everything would be so hot, fast, and energetic that they would likely live thousands of generations in just minutes of our time. The organisms would be flatter than a sheet of paper, crushed by 100 billion times more gravity than we have on Earth.

If intelligent life ever evolved on a neutron star, they would probably think that water-based life was a ridiculous idea. Frankly, they'd likely have no idea what water even was.

❖ STRINGS INSIDE STARS

One of the most mind-blowing ideas of life in the universe came from a 2020 study by Luis Anchordoqui and Eugene Chudnovsky.

Inside stars, the environment is pretty hot. Atoms of hydrogen are tossed around as they get smashed into helium. Everything is a soupy plasma of particles that slosh around at close to 15 million degrees Celsius. But stars might also contain objects that literally break the universe: *magnetic monopoles* and *cosmic strings*.

Here's where things get a bit stringy.

When space collapsed as our universe was born, it might not have settled exactly the same everywhere, so we might have been left with many regions of space that had slightly different properties, all splotched in a mess across the cosmos.

In certain places, weird objects called monopoles might have appeared. Magnetic monopoles are charged particles that either attract or repel, but not both. That's something we've never seen a magnet do before, but the laws of physics don't explicitly say they can't exist.

Right at the border between two slightly different regions of space, we might get wacky objects called cosmic strings. They're like the stitches between two fabrics that have been sewed together. Again, we've never seen them, but physics hasn't said they can't exist.

If these strings settled in the cores of giant stars, the sloshing plasma might have caused them to get tangled up and stretched. If magnetic monopoles fell into stars, they'd be tossed around by the magnetically charged plasma. The coolest bit is that these strings and monopoles could join together, forming long chains and strands. If it ever evolved into a hot and electric sort of life, it would definitely qualify as one of the most exotic species in the entire universe.

Such weird forms of life would literally eat hydrogen plasma as it fused and smashed into helium. The energy of nuclear fusion would be enough to keep these organisms alive. They would have absolutely nothing in common with us, and yet, amazingly, they could evolve in the same way we did.

Cosmic strings and monopoles would randomly stretch and shuffle until they fell into a shape that could make more copies of itself. The combinations that made better stringy structures would survive and reproduce. The combinations that did poorly would disintegrate. Natural selection could be the one thing we share with life across the entire cosmos.

All of this is sheer speculation, but cosmic-string-based life in the core of a star just goes to show that life could exist in places that we blatantly overlook in our search for life in space.

❖ OUR ARBITRARY EXISTENCE

We're on the frontier of an ongoing process called life. It's been going nonstop for almost four billion years on

Earth, and it's quite possible that the game of life has been playing out across the universe for nearly fourteen billion years.

Faced with the incredible range of living things that could evolve across the cosmos, we seem to just be a byproduct of our planet. We're made of the exact same stuff that makes up the stars and galaxies, just rearranged in an intricate way. Our arrangement is brief, temporary, and fleeting. Entropy eventually does its thing.

Life may just be a byproduct of our universe, but we shouldn't feel worthless. Intelligent life has a property that the rest of the universe doesn't: we're aware of our surroundings. We don't really know how consciousness works, and it doesn't fit any agreed upon scientific theory. Our brains really should be unaware, since they're just a huge collection of little particles obeying the laws of physics. But that's not what happens; for some weird and wacky reason, we're actually aware of ourselves. We can experience reality. For a bunch of dead cosmic matter, that's pretty special.

The hundred billion billion billion subatomic particles in your body used to be scattered across the universe. Against all odds, they're all now in the same place. They're making up a brain that's reading about its own existence. They're contemplating the universe from which they came. For a lack of better words, that's pretty freaking awesome.

If life didn't exist, the universe would still go on as usual. Ten septillion planets would keep orbiting their stars. Waves would keep crashing on shores across the cosmos. Clouds would keep dancing across the skies of alien worlds. Galaxies would keep twirling, and the stars would keep shining. But without life, all those marvels would be appreciated by no one.

Here we are, alive, in this universe. We can stand on the surface of our planet and gaze upward into the sky. We're a small part of the cosmos staring, in awe, at itself. That's just life.

PART 6

DOWN TO EARTH

THE REASON TO KEEP LOOKING UP

We've just checked out the shallows of what will surely turn out to be an ocean of cosmic mysteries. Humanity has a long way to go before we've figured it all out. Is the universe infinite in size, or could we reach the end? Did we come from the epic collapse of space itself, or did we come from a random burst of energy within an older, dead, and empty universe? Is our strain of life really the only one possible, or could there be creatures of silicon right underneath us? Why do some people pour the milk first and then add the cereal?

Many of these questions are nearly solved, but others are still obscure, or impossible to conceive of at the moment. There are so many fascinating parts of our universe that are still waiting to be probed in search of answers, and even if we discover those answers, we'll likely find a thousand new questions to ask.

Just searching for the truth, for answers to the biggest questions in the universe, and for the delicious bits of knowledge that make our minds crave more, is enough to make us feel like we're not entirely missing out.

We *are* missing out on a whole lot, though.

The universe is the ultimate source of FOMO (fear of missing out) for curious minds of all ages, and since we're confined to such a small corner of a huge and vast universe, it leaves us with a burning thirst for knowing more about the cosmos around us. Even just grasping a tiny fraction of the wonders of our universe is enough to quench that thirst. For now, at least.

ONE LITTLE PLANET

Let's not sugarcoat the obvious: our planet is fragile. It's perched at the edge of our star's habitable zone. An asteroid the size of Mount Everest—which, in comparison to Earth, would be like comparing a basketball and a speck of dust—is enough to wipe out all life on this planet. Meanwhile, we possess enough nuclear weapons to destroy every city on Earth and send the whole planet into a global decades-long winter.

It's unfortunate that we are so obsessed with arming our planet against itself, rather than looking outward toward the universe and the future of the human race.

❖ WE ARE EARTHLINGS

If everyone on this planet could see us from the perspective of the universe, perhaps we'd think differently. Maybe the people waging wars and conflicts would reconsider how much the capturing of oil, territory, or population actually means in the big picture. Maybe the haters of races and religions would realize that we share the exact same origins, are made of the same atoms, and are all doomed to the exact same cosmic fate. Perhaps the leaders of fossil fuel industries would see that our planet is fragile, coated in a thin atmosphere of air that is delicately keeping the world alive every single day.

When we see the true smallness and vulnerability of Earth, it feels so obvious that wars must end, that climate change should be stopped at all costs, that every person on this planet should get along with one another, and that everyone should do what they want with their lives and be exactly who they want to be.

But we're not there yet.

❖ THE FINITE CLIMATE

The rise of sea levels feels slow when spread across the world's oceans; it's easy to ignore it completely. But if you were to divert the melting ice into a ten-metre-wide circular tunnel instead, it would fill with water at a rate of about 300 metres per second. That's fast enough to reach the edge of space in five minutes.

Carbon emissions don't seem so massive because our atmosphere can hold huge clouds and blow plumes away in the wind. Yes, our atmosphere is enormous, but it definitely isn't endless. If we were to convert atmospheric carbon emissions into their equivalent weight in graphite carbon pencils, based on emission rates from the Second International Conference on Negative CO_2 Emissions held in Sweden in 2022, the entire island of Manhattan would be blanketed in pencils to a depth of one kilometre after just 180 days.

A year is a very long unit of time, so it's hard to grasp it in the moment. But based on a paper published in 2012 in *Global Perspectives on Sustainable Forest Management*, a square kilometre of trees are destroyed, burned, and cut down every ten minutes. Consider the irony of publishing a *paper* on that topic in the first place.

It's a matter of perspective.

The example of the planet Venus is a terrifying possibility for the Earth's future. Around four billion years ago, it likely resembled our Earth, with lush oceans and a cooler temperature. But as water and carbon dioxide filled the atmosphere, it trapped more of the Sun's heat, boiling water and choking the atmosphere, setting off a runaway cycle. Now Venus is a dead inferno.

The universe contains too many examples of planets that never made it.

❖ A WORLD WITHOUT BORDERS

Think of how familiar it is to turn on the news and hear about nations arguing over borders, resources, and money. Why exactly are we doing these things? When you throw it into cosmic perspective, every battle in the history of the world was just DNA killing DNA in a universe that never altered in the slightest—regardless of who won or who lost.

By the time World War I came to an end in 1918, 22 million people had been killed. The German border had been pushed 100 kilometres west into France, but eight months after the war ended, the Treaty of Versailles undid that progression and returned the borders to their prewar state. As the crushed Ottoman Empire was divvied up to the rest of Europe, new borders and boundaries were drawn around the people and territories of the Middle East. This redrawing of lines and borders and shifting of centres of power led to an estimated 18 million deaths from conflicts that brewed and erupted over the next century. Frankly, it truly crossed the line.

At the time of writing, the Russo-Ukrainian War is killing thousands of people and costing 900 million dollars every day to cover the cost of attacks and reparations, the medical emergencies, and the development of weapons on both sides. If that massive volume of money were directed toward space exploration rather than international conflict, we could literally launch an entire Apollo moon mission on a Saturn-V rocket every 36 hours.

So, why do people do this? There has to be a reason.

❖ NOT DYING TODAY

If we were fine with dying today, we would've gone extinct millions of years ago. It's a simple truth: if a species is afraid of dying, it adds an incentive to make copies of itself so the species can live on. It's natural for us to be at least a little worried about dying. Those species who were fine with dying, well… *died*.

Having babies is how we, as a species, keep our genetic code alive. We take the information in our DNA and cut-and-paste it into another living organism that'll live longer than us. If you die with nothing to remember you by, then it's as if you never existed. Maybe you're fine with that; maybe you're haunted by it.

How do we keep a part of ourselves alive after we die? One way is to build a legacy. We do things that impact other people; we want to leave a mark on the world. The same impetus can drive wars between nations, or drive a global effort against climate change. It inspires us to make art, start businesses, and speak out. It's that little urge to stay alive even after your physical body falls apart. It's exactly how DNA's been doing it for almost four billion years—and it's gotten really good at it.

It's like evolution, but instead of species competing to fill an ecosystem with their genetic code, it's fellow humans competing to fill the future of humanity with their particular mindset and their vision.

There's no rulebook, other than the one we might invent for ourselves, of course. There's no law of physics stopping us from doing whatever we choose on this planet—except time travel to the past.

How would you like the future to progress?

THE POINT OF IT ALL

We only arrived on the cosmic stage after 99.998% of our universe's history had already played out. If our species survives as long as the average mammal does, we'll be around for an additional 0.007% of that cosmic history before we fizzle out of existence.

If we make an international truce and end all future conflict, rapidly mobilize to stop the climate crisis, and break free from the bounds of our planet, perhaps we'll set sail into a universe that will eventually freeze forever and crumble into nothingness. So, why would we do that? Why do we climb mountains? Why do we go *anywhere*?

Everything we do in the brief time we have in this universe—all the people we meet and love and hate, all the things we accomplish and achieve, all the jokes we tell, all the pranks we play, all the work we put into our lives, all the knowledge we gain, all the lessons we learn, all the memories we make, and all the good we do in the world—will get thrown into a dissolving cosmic soup and become permanently erased.

So, does any of it matter?

❖ DOES IT MATTER?

To be honest, if you were *really* looking for an optimistic answer to this, you should have chosen a different book.

The cosmos is so much bigger than our one little planet. We could literally vanish from existence and the rest of the universe would go on, completely oblivious.

As soon as the universe drains all the meaning and purpose out of us, something feels a little bit violated. Searching for truth and meaning is very human in nature. Our species might disagree on the most ridiculous things, but one thing we all share is a desire for meaning and purpose.

But that's the one thing we don't seem to have in this universe.

In the most literal sense, we're a collection of atoms that simply became aware of themselves. Those atoms came from the cores of exploding stars, which in turn came from the blazing birth of our universe, which happened for no reason other than a little random fluctuation in space itself.

Our atoms will keep existing for trillions of years after their brief time in a human body is over. When we look around us, we see an environment that's perfect for human life. We might think the Earth and the universe were serendipitously made just for us, but we forget that we'd be making the exact same assumption if we were any other intelligent species on any other planet in any other universe.

All the laws of society were made by humans operating on the rules of biology, which operates on the rules of chemistry, which operates on the laws of physics, which is not much more than plain math.

Why does a chemical reaction happen? Why do particle collisions happen? Why does math happen? Our existence doesn't seem to have a grandiose meaning or purpose: it just sort of happened. It seems a little pointless to figure out *why* it happened.

But isn't it incredible that we can figure out *how* it happened?

❖ THE COSMIC LOTTERY

Hey, at least we exist in the first place. We won the cosmic lottery.

When our universe was born, its space collapsed out of the rapidly expanding void of inflation. It settled into the kind of space that we live in, containing the laws of physics that we're familiar with. It could have collapsed into trillions of other possible versions of space and physics.

The total number of other possibilities, calculated by Andrei Linde and Vitaly Vanchurin, is around ten quadrillion orders of magnitude larger than the number of atoms in our universe. None of those alternate realities would be anything like this one. When tiny particles of matter finally appeared out of the firestorm of the Big Bang, they could have appeared in any one of 10^{115}

possible arrangements besides this one, and none of them would have led to this exact universe.

Out of two trillion galaxies, a septillion stars, and up to ten septillion planets, here we are on Earth. Our entire solar system most likely formed when the shockwave of an exploding supernova swept through a cloud of dust in deep space, causing it to collapse. If a star hadn't exploded in our vicinity some five billion years ago, our entire solar system wouldn't even exist.

A rainy day might sound miserable, but we have the luxury of living on the only planet within 400 trillion kilometres where liquid water falls from the sky. The nearest rainy worlds are most likely the third, fourth, and fifth planets in the TRAPPIST-1 system, 39 light-years from home.

We live right in the middle of the age of starlight in this universe. Life is only possible for the first 100 trillion years of cosmic history, which is an awesomely tiny window of time. Our universe will keep evolving for a billion trillion trillion trillion trillion trillion trillion times longer than that brief window. Today is just one day in the 1,752,000,000,000 days of Earth's history that have gone by so far.

Our brains grew to their full size thanks to one single genetic mutation: a swapping of just one cytosine molecule. That mutation could have been caused by something as tiny as a single subatomic particle blasted out of a supernova explosion. Perhaps a star exploded and launched gamma rays in all directions, and a hundred million years later, one of those particles struck a chunk of our DNA inside a reproductive cell in a primate of ours. Every human brain in existence owes its intelligence directly to that one mutation, caused by such an absurd fluke that nobody would have ever suspected that the entire future of our planet depended on it. That single piece of DNA led to a global civilization, the rapid changing of Earth's climate, and the evolution of a species with the brilliant potential to explore the universe. We need to remember how unimaginably unlikely our existence is in the first place.

If we want to write out all the zeroes in the absurd probability of us existing, at this text size, we would need around 10 trillion sheets of paper.

In a hundred quadrillion years, the place you're sitting right now will be an empty vacuum filled with a few decaying particles. In a bleak way, it's comforting to know that our universe exists for so much more than just us. Honestly, if the cosmos existed solely for us, it'd be a literal waste of space.

In some ways, it's nice to know that nothing we do will ever really change the outcome of the universe. We're on a wild ride through space and time on our spaceship Earth, and if none of it means anything in the big picture, we're forced to find meaning in the little things. In a universe where nothing actually makes a difference, we get to decide what's meaningful to us.

The awesome size of the universe tosses us into a place where we feel kind of like nothing, but at the same time, it pulls us back to our little place on Earth and allows us to focus on the smaller things that matter most.

THE REASON TO KNOW

Despite the amazing feelings of awe that these discoveries give us, many would argue that there's no point in searching for our origin story, life in space, or distant galaxies—that it's a waste of money that could otherwise be put toward the actual development of our civilization. They have a point: our modern society doesn't depend on distant galaxies to function.

So, what's the point of trying to uncover our distant origins, looking abstractly far into the future, searching the galaxy for alien life, or imagining past the edge of our universe? With all the money and effort needed for this kind of research, why do we care about knowing these things?

The human species is a small part of an amazing and beautiful story. It's the story of the evolution of life, the universe's explosive origin and freezing death, from the smallest particles to the biggest galaxies. At the present moment, we're just a footnote in that story. We might not always be, depending on how far we go, but for now, we really are a cosmic speck.

❖ KEEP LOOKING UP

Even if we're ridiculously small in the bigger picture, we're capable of seeing that picture, and perhaps that awareness can make us a better species too. It's so easy to lose ourselves in the giant society we've built around us. Going to university or college, getting a good job, making a living, and buying a house are all things people do to succeed in the system we've created, but none of those are universal laws that existed before we came along. None of society's rules existed before humanity, that's for sure.

Given that most of us are busy just living, why would we care about distant galaxies, absurd alien life forms, our cosmic origin story, or the ultimate fate?

It keeps us looking up as a species.

It reminds us that we haven't got it all figured out.

When all of human society gets reduced to something so absurdly small in the bigger picture, it dares us to challenge the status quo. It makes us question the things we usually take for granted. It makes us doubt the rules that everyone seems to go along with. It reminds us that nothing's set in stone, nothing will last forever, and change is inevitable. It nudges us to rise up against some of the nearsighted things our species has decided to do.

War is so profitable and nationalism so powerful, but these things are futile and meaningless in the huge void of intergalactic space. Coal and fossil fuel industries are so successful in this society because of the profit they generate, but as soon as we realize that money is *also* a thing we invented ourselves, it becomes quickly obvious that we're caught in our own net.

When we realize that society was established *by* people *for* people—not a set of cosmic rules that were always in place—it lets us take a step back and realize what actually matters to us and the rest of humanity. Seeing the bigger picture is what drives change. It's what channels the passion of humanity into something really meaningful.

❖ OUR PURPOSE

If none of this feels right to you, then heck, we can invent a grandiose cosmic purpose for ourselves if we want.

Perhaps we exist for the purpose of figuring out the universe around us. It's what all of us have been doing since the day we were born, and no matter where we are in society, we keep doing it.

A scientist running an experiment, a businessperson looking at how customers interact, a programmer creating new software, an engineer testing a prototype, a chef whisking up a new recipe, an artist trying out a new medium—that's curiosity. Any time you've ever asked a question about even the smallest thing—that's curiosity. Any random internet search or shiny object that catches your eye—that's curiosity too.

It's when you're looking at the stubby wings of an airplane and wondering how it's even possible that it flies. It's when you're looking at the slab rock tiles on the floor and seeing ten million years of Earth's history beneath your feet. It's when a bug lands on you and you don't shake it off because you want to watch it walk around. It's when you tilt your head at night to see how you're oriented relative to other objects in universe. It's curiosity.

Without curiosity, humanity is just existing to keep existing. Curiosity may have killed the cat, but with all due respect, the cat was going to die anyway.

Maybe the human brain isn't much. After all, it's just a lump of meat, folded and creased and intertwined with blood vessels, consisting of a hundred billion little neurons. However, these lumps of meat invented neuroscience and had the wild idea of studying themselves. Human brains managed to crack the chemical code of rocket fuel and used it to propel themselves off of their planet and into the universe from which they came. Human brains invented stories.

Our little minds aren't much in comparison to massive stars and galaxies, but our ability to contemplate things is impressive. If a typical thought lasts for one second, then the total number of possible thoughts we are capable of stirring up in our lifetime is about 200 trillion orders of magnitude larger than the number of atoms in the entire observable universe.

Not bad for a kilogram of cells. Not bad at all.

ACKNOWLEDGEMENTS

It has always been one of my dreams to publish a book. It's true that I wouldn't be here without the Big Bang, the formation of the Earth, the origin of prebiotic life in the early oceans, and the random mutations that led to the evolution of the human race—but I would also like to thank the *people* who have made this book possible.

I'm very grateful for the patience and support provided to me by my friends and family. I'd like to thank my sister, Tess, for waiting to play the violin until after my writer's block had passed. I'd like to thank my parents for their endless feedback, and for their generous sacrifices of food as I parasitically feasted off their fridge. I am indebted to the Nerd Cult of the Mount Douglas Challenge Program— my classmates, in essence—for their support while I was juggling this book and my academic commitments. I'm grateful to Ted Meldrum and Shona Lindsay for their support and guidance in writing this book.

I would like to extend a huge thanks to Dr. Georgia G. Soares (Postdoc, Geosciences, Penn State University) for kindly reviewing and proofreading my research on the origin of life on Earth and elsewhere. I should have known—that's just life. I would like to extend another huge thanks to Simon Smith (MSc, Astronomy, University of Victoria) for proofreading my research on astrophysics, galaxies, and the stupendous scale of the universe. I appreciate your enthusiasm on the colossal size of our galactic supercluster.

Thank you to Neal Johnson, my fabulous math and science teacher, for always being willing to chat with me after school about the weirdest scientific problems. Thank you for keeping the Nerd Cult alive, and for reading my various writings before I even had the idea of making a book. I am grateful for your feedback, and, of course, your permission for me to use some of your legendary science humour in the manuscript. Thank you to Anna Kratofil for reading over the manuscript to make sure my writing still sounded human. Thank you for catching when my deep existentialism went too far. Thank you to Joanne Kettner for looking over my writing on infinite universes and very large numbers. I appreciate your advice on how to compile a scientific textbook—it helped me decide not to write one—and your feedback on my writing.

This book has changed a lot since I first started writing it, and the process has turned out to be more excitingly complicated than I could have possibly imagined. In guiding me through the wild ride of publishing a book, I am grateful to my publisher, Linda Leith, and my loyal editors Leila Marshy, Jennifer McMorran, Edward He, Christina Soubassakou, and Shakiya Williams, and designer Debbie Geltner. Thank you for taking on the admirable task of turning these words into a book and making my idea a reality. It means the world to me—and frankly a good portion of the observable universe too.

I would like to express my gratitude to the Victoria Centre of the Royal Astronomical Society of Canada, for whose support, passion, and opportunities I cannot thank them enough. From summer Saturday night star parties up at the observatory, to Monday evenings at Astronomy Café, to helping me get involved with *SkyNews* magazine, you welcomed me and opened up my universe. For that I'm eternally grateful.

I would like to thank Carl Sagan for being awesome, and for being my inspiration since I was five years old. I would also like to thank Isaac Newton, Marie Curie, Albert Einstein, Henrietta Swan Leavitt, Stephen Hawking, Vera Rubin, Edwin Hubble, Aristotle, Claudius Ptolemy, Galileo Galilei, Nicolaus Copernicus, Lord Kelvin, Johannes Kepler, Max Planck, Antonie van Leeuwenhoek, Ludwig Boltzmann, Charles Darwin, Dmitri Mendeleev, Rosalind Franklin, Robert Hooke, and everyone who has contributed to our modern understanding of the universe. A huge thanks to these folks, seriously—I couldn't have written this book without them.

FURTHER READING

Adams, Fred C. "The Degree of Fine-Tuning in Our Universe — and Others." Physics Reports, vol. 807, May 2019, pp. 1–111. https://doi.org/10.1016/j.physrep.2019.02.001.

Allahverdi, R., Brandenberger, R., Cyr-Racine, F.-Y., and Mazumdar, A. (2010). Reheating in Inflationary Cosmology: Theory and Applications. *Annual Review of Nuclear and Particle Science*. 60. 27–51. https://doi.org/10.1146/annurev.nucl.012809.104511

Altwegg K., et al. Prebiotic chemicals-amino acid and phosphorus-in the coma of comet 67P/Churyumov-Gerasimenko. Sci Adv. 2016 May 27;2(5):e1600285. doi: 10.1126/sciadv.1600285. PMID: 27386550; PMCID: PMC4928965.

Attwater J., Raguram A., Morgunov A. S., Gianni E., Holliger P. Ribozyme-catalysed RNA synthesis using triplet building blocks. Elife. 2018 May 15;7:e35255. doi: 10.7554/eLife.35255. PMID: 29759114; PMCID: PMC6003772.

Baland, R. M., et al. "Titan's Obliquity as Evidence of a Subsurface Ocean?" Astronomy & Astrophysics, vol. 530, May 2011, p. A141. Crossref, https://doi.org/10.1051/0004-6361/201116578.

Bandari, A. (2022, November 29). *No Phosphine on Venus, According to SOFIA – SOFIA: Stratospheric Observatory for Infrared Astronomy*. NASA Blogs. Retrieved August 18, 2023, from https://blogs.nasa.gov/sofia/2022/11/29/no-phosphine-on-venus-according-to-sofia/

Bar-Yosef, O. (1998). The Natufian Culture in the Levant, Threshold to the Origins of Agriculture. *Evolutionary Anthropology*, 159–173. http://www.columbia.edu/itc/anthropology/v1007/baryo.pdf

Bennett, C., et al. (2012). Nine-Year Wilkinson Microwave Anisotropy Probe (WMAP) Observations: Final Maps and Results.

The Astrophysical Journal Supplement Series. 208. 10.1088/0067-0049/208/2/20.

Bennett, C. L., et al. (2013). "Nine-Year Wilkinson Microwave Anisotropy Probe (WMAP) Observations: Final Maps and Results". *Astrophysical Journal Supplement*. 208 (2): 20. arXiv:1212.5225. Bibcode:2013ApJS..208...20B. doi:10.1088/0067-0049/208/2/20. S2CID 119271232.

Berardelli, J., & Niemczyk, K. (2021, March 4). *The Great Dying: Earth's largest-ever mass extinction is a warning for humanity*. CBS News. Retrieved August 18, 2023, from https://www.cbsnews.com/news/great-dying-permian-triassic-extinction-event-warning-humanity/#textThe20worst20came20a20littleof20life20on20land-20vanished

Bland-Hawthorn, J. & Gerhard, O. (2016). The Galaxy in Context: Structural, Kinematic, and Integrated Properties. *Annual Review of Astronomy and Astrophysics*. 54: 529–596.

Boss, Alan P., and Sandra A. Keiser. "Triggering Collapse of the Presolar Dense Cloud Core and Injecting Short-lived Radioisotopes with a Shock Wave. II. Varied Shock Wave and Cloud Core Parameters." The Astrophysical Journal, vol. 770, no. 1, May 2013, p. 51. Crossref, https://doi.org/10.1088/0004-637x/770/1/51.

Bray, Dennis. *Cell Movements*. New York: Garland, 1992: 6.

Briggs, A. (2023, February 7). *The asteroid belt contains solar system remnants*. EarthSky. Retrieved May 28, 2023, from https://earthsky.org/space/what-is-the-asteroid-belt/

Briggs, John C. "Emergence of a sixth mass extinction?" *Biological Journal of the Linnean Society*, vol. 122, no. 2, 2017, pp. 243–248, https://doi.org/10.1093/biolinnean/blx063.

Brouillette, M. (2022, April 19). *How Did Life Spring Up From Non-Life? Scientists May Finally Have Some Clues*. Popular Mechanics.

Retrieved August 18, 2023, from https://www.popularmechanics. com/science/a39762892/how-did-life-spring-up-from-non-life/

Brouillette, M. (2022, April 19). How Did Life Spring Up From Non-Life? Scientists May Finally Have Some Clues. Popular Mechanics. Retrieved May 4, 2023, from https://www.popularme-chanics.com/science/a39762892/how-did-life-spring-up-from-non-life/

Brown, Dwayne, and Cathy Weselby. "NASA - NASA-Funded Research Discovers Life Built With Toxic Chemical." NASA - Home. NASA, 02 Dec. 2010. Web. 18 Oct. 2011. http://www.nasa.gov/ topics/universe/features/astrobiology_toxic_chemical.html

Camacho-Quevedo, Benjamin, and Enrique Gaztañaga. "A Measurement of the Scale of Homogeneity in the Early Universe." Journal of Cosmology and Astroparticle Physics, vol. 2022, no. 04, Apr. 2022, p. 044. Crossref, https://doi.org/10.1088/1475-7516/ 2022/04/044.

Camilo Mora, Derek P. Tittensor, Sina Adl, Alastair G. B. Simpson, Boris Worm. How Many Species Are There on Earth and in the Ocean? *PLoS Biology*, 2011; 9 (8): e1001127 DOI: 10.1371/journal. pbio.1001127

Cartwright, A. (2016). The Venus Hypothesis. arXiv: Earth and Planetary Astrophysics.

Cavalier-Smith T. Origin of mitochondria by intracellular enslave-ment of a photosynthetic purple bacterium. Proc Biol Sci. 2006 Aug 7;273(1596):1943–52. doi: 10.1098/rspb.2006.3531. PMID: 16822756; PMCID: PMC1634775.

Cavailier-Smith, Thomas. (2006). Origin of mitochondria by intracellular enslavement of a photosynthetic purple bacterium. Proceedings. Biological sciences / The Royal Society. 273. 1943–52. 10.1098/rspb.2006.3531.

Census of Marine Life. "How many species on Earth? About 8.7 million, new estimate says." ScienceDaily. ScienceDaily, 24 August 2011. www.sciencedaily.com/releases/2011/08/110823180459.htm

Chakravarty, Sumit, et al. "Deforestation: Causes, Effects and Control Strategies." 2012, https://cdn.intechopen.com/pdfs/36125/InTech-Deforestation_causes_effects_and_control_strategies.pdf. Accessed 4 May 2023.

Chapter 1 Organic Compounds: Alkanes Organic chemistry nowadays almost drives me mad. To me it appears like a primeval tropical. (n.d.). Angelo State University. Retrieved August 18, 2023, from https://www.angelo.edu/faculty/kboudrea/index_2353/Chapter_01_2SPP.pdf

Cherry, K. (2021, November 19). Action Potential and How Neurons Fire. Verywell Mind. Retrieved May 4, 2023, from https://www.verywellmind.com/what-is-an-action-potential-2794811

Choi S., Meyer M. O., Bevilacqua P. C., Keating C. D. Phase-specific RNA accumulation and duplex thermodynamics in multiphase coacervate models for membraneless organelles. Nat Chem. 2022 Oct;14(10):1110–1117. doi: 10.1038/s41557-022-00980-7. Epub 2022 Jun 30. PMID: 35773489.

Choi, C. Q. (2017, February 13). *How Did Multicellular Life Evolve? | News | Astrobiology*. NASA Astrobiology. Retrieved August 18, 2023, from https://astrobiology.nasa.gov/news/how-did-multicellular-life-evolve/

Clement Akais, Okia. Global Perspectives on Sustainable Forest Management. InTech. 2012.

Cochrane, C. J., et al. "In Search of Subsurface Oceans Within the Uranian Moons." Journal of Geophysical Research: Planets, vol. 126, no. 12, Dec. 2021. Portico, Crossref, https://doi.org/10.1029/2021je006956.

Cojocaru, R., & Fraser, S. (2017, November 1). *Origin of life: Transitioning to DNA genomes in an RNA world*. eLife. Retrieved August 18, 2023, from https://elifesciences.org/articles/32330

Cold Case: Possible Ice Volcano on Titan. (2022, September 27). National Geographic Society. Retrieved May 28, 2023, from https://education.nationalgeographic.org/resource/cold-case-possible-ice-volcano-titan/

Cosmic Microwave Background Dipole | COSMOS. (n.d.). Centre for Astrophysics and Supercomputing. Retrieved August 18, 2023, from https://astronomy.swin.edu.au/cosmos/c/Cosmic+Microwave+Background+Dipole

Costanzo, V. (n.d.). *Life on a Neutron Star: An Interview With Frank Drake*. Gwern. Retrieved August 18, 2023, from https://gwern.net/doc/science/1973-drake.pdf

Could silicon be the basis for alien life forms, just as carbon is on Earth? (1998, February 23). Scientific American. Retrieved May 28, 2023, from https://www.scientificamerican.com/article/could-silicon-be-the-basi/

Cowen, R. Voyager 1 has reached interstellar space. *Nature* (2013). https://doi.org/10.1038/nature.2013.13735

Damer B. & Deamer D. The Hot Spring Hypothesis for an Origin of Life. Astrobiology. 2020 Apr;20(4):429–452. doi: 10.1089/ast.2019.2045. Epub 2019 Dec 16. PMID: 31841362; PMCID: PMC7133448.

De Sanctis, M. C., Ammannito, E., Raponi, A. et al. Fresh emplacement of hydrated sodium chloride on Ceres from ascending salty fluids. *Nat Astron* 4, 786–793 (2020). https://doi.org/10.1038/s41550-020-1138-8

Deamer D. Origins of Life Research: The Conundrum between Laboratory and Field Simulations of Messy Environments. Life

(Basel). 2022 Sep 14;12(9):1429. doi: 10.3390/life12091429. PMID: 36143465; PMCID: PMC9504664.

Deason, Alis J., et al. "The Edge of the Galaxy." Monthly Notices of the Royal Astronomical Society, vol. 496, no. 3, June 2020, pp. 3929–42. Crossref, https://doi.org/10.1093/mnras/staa1711.

Devlin, H. (2020, February 27). *Biggest cosmic explosion ever detected left huge dent in space.* The Guardian. Retrieved August 18, 2023, from https://www.theguardian.com/science/2020/feb/27/biggest-cosmic-explosion-ever-detected-makes-huge-dent-in-space

Did Ancient Eruptions Form Life's Building Blocks? (2011, March 25). NPR. Retrieved August 18, 2023, from https://www.npr.org/

Discovery of "Arsenic-bug" Expands Definition of Life | Science Mission Directorate. (2010, December 2). NASA Science. Retrieved May 28, 2023, from https://science.nasa.gov/science-news/science-at-nasa/2010/02dec_monolake

Donau, C., Späth, F., Sosson, M. et al. Active coacervate droplets as a model for membraneless organelles and protocells. *Nat Commun* 11, 5167 (2020). https://doi.org/10.1038/s41467-020-18815-9

Doyle, B. (2017, December 3). Look who breathed the same air we breathe. Cumberland Times-News. Retrieved May 4, 2023, from https://www.times-news.com/opinion/look-who-breathed-the-same-air-we-breathe/article_67ab981c-d6d7-11e7-ad3b-276bac78160d.html

Drahl, C. (2012, January 23). *Arsenic-Based-Life-Aftermath.* C&EN. Retrieved August 18, 2023, from https://cen.acs.org/articles/90/web/2012/01/Arsenic-Based-Life-Aftermath.html

Dressler, A. "The Great Attractor: do galaxies trace the large-scale mass distribution?" *Nature* 350, 391–397 (1991). https://doi.org/10.1038/350391a0

Dunn J, Grider M. H. Physiology, Adenosine Triphosphate. [Updated 2023 Feb 13]. In: StatPearls [Internet]. Treasure Island (FL): StatPearls Publishing; 2023 Jan-. Available from: https://www.ncbi.nlm.nih.gov/books/NBK553175/

Edwards, Gordon. "Health and Environmental Issues Linked to the Nuclear Fuel Chain." *Health/Environment Issues Linked to the Nuclear Fuel Chain — Section B*, Canadian Environmental Advisory Council, http://www.ccnr.org/CEAC_B.html. Accessed 4 May 2023.

Eicher, D. J. (2019, July 1). "Did Comets Bring Life to Earth?" | *Astronomy.com*. Astronomy Magazine. Retrieved August 18, 2023, from https://www.astronomy.com/science/did-comets-bring-life-to-earth/

Erlich, Y., & Zielinski, D. (2017, March 3). "DNA Fountain enables a robust and efficient storage architecture." *Science.* Retrieved May 4, 2023, from https://www.science.org/doi/10.1126/science.aaj2038

ESA - Dwarf galaxies around the Milky Way. (n.d.). European Space Agency. Retrieved May 28, 2023, from https://www.esa.int/ESA_Multimedia/Images/2021/11/Dwarf_galaxies_around_the_Milky_Way

Evidence of Cryovolcanism on Titan | U.S. Geological Survey. (2018, October 24). USGS.gov. Retrieved May 28, 2023, from https://www.usgs.gov/centers/astrogeology-science-center/science/evidence-cryovolcanism-tita

Exoplanet Catalog | Discovery – Exoplanet Exploration: Planets Beyond our Solar System. (n.d.). Exoplanet Exploration. Retrieved May 28, 2023, from https://exoplanets.nasa.gov/discovery/exoplanet-catalog/

Faculty of Physics University of Warsaw. (2018, June 7). "Dark inflation opens up a gravitational window onto the first moments after the Big Bang." *ScienceDaily*. Retrieved April 2, 2023, from https://www.sciencedaily.com/releases/2018/06/180607100920.htm

Fekry, Mostafa & Tipton, Peter & Gates, Kent. (2011). Kinetic Consequences of Replacing the Internucleotide Phosphorus Atoms in DNA with Arsenic. ACS chemical biology. 6. 127–30.

Flam, F. (2012, July 16). *Studies dispel claims of 'shadow biosphere' on Earth*. Phys.org. Retrieved May 28, 2023, from https://phys.org/news/2012-07-dispel-shadow-biosphere-earth.html

Florio M., Namba T., Pääbo S., Hiller M., Huttner W. B.. A single splice site mutation in human-specific *ARHGAP11B* causes basal progenitor amplification. Sci Adv. 2016 Dec 7;2(12):e1601941. doi: 10.1126/sciadv.1601941. PMID: 27957544; PMCID: PMC5142801.

Fortes, A. D. (2000). "Exobiological implications of a possible ammonia-water ocean inside Titan". *Icarus*. 146 (2): 444–452.

Reiss, A. G., Yuan, W., Macri, L. M., et al. (2022). A Comprehensive Measurement of the Local Value of the Hubble Constant with 1 km s^{-1} Mpc^{-1} Uncertainty from the Hubble Space Telescope and the SH0ES Team. https://arxiv.org/pdf/2112.04510.pdf

Gelvin, J. L. (2005). The Israel-Palestine Conflict: One Hundred Years of War. Cambridge University Press.

Giacintucci, S., et al. "Discovery of a Giant Radio Fossil in the Ophiuchus Galaxy Cluster." The Astrophysical Journal, vol. 891, no. 1, Feb. 2020, p. 1. Crossref, https://doi.org/10.3847/1538-4357/ab6a9d.

Gohd, C. (2021, April 14). *Did lightning help spark life on Earth?* Space.com. Retrieved August 18, 2023, from https://www.space.com/life-on-earth-sparked-by-lightning

Greaves, J.S., Richards, A.M.S., Bains, W. et al. Phosphine gas in the cloud decks of Venus. *Nat Astron* 5, 655–664 (2021). https://doi.org/10.1038/s41550-020-1174-4

Guth, A. (1997). The Inflationary Universe. Basic Books.

Hallsworth, J.E., Koop, T., Dallas, T.D. et al. Water activity in Venus's uninhabitable clouds and other planetary atmospheres. *Nat Astron* 5, 665–675 (2021). https://doi.org/10.1038/s41550-021-01391-3

Harris, William E. (February 2003). "Catalog of Parameters for Milky Way Globular Clusters: The Database" (text). SEDS. Archived from the original on March 9, 2012. Retrieved May 10, 2007.

Haynes, K. (2019, August 15). "New date for 'Late Heavy Bombardment' may change life's timeline on Earth" *Astronomy.com.* Astronomy Magazine. Retrieved August 18, 2023, from https://www.astronomy.com/science/new-date-for-late-heavy-bombardment-may-change-lifes-timeline-on-earth/

Hellingwerf, K. J., Crielaard, W., and Westerhoff, H. V. (1993). "Comparison of Retinal-Based and Chlorophyll-Based Photosynthesis: A Biothermokinetic Description of Photochemical Reaction Centers". *Modern Trends in Biothermokinetics.* pp. 45–52. doi:10.1007/978-1-4615-2962-0_9. ISBN 978-1-4613-6288-3.

Helmenstine, A. M. (2019, April 5). "How Many Atoms Are in the Human Body?" *ThoughtCo.* Retrieved May 4, 2023, from https://www.thoughtco.com/how-many-atoms-are-in-human-body-603872

Hess, B.L., Piazolo, S. & Harvey, J. "Lightning strikes as a major facilitator of prebiotic phosphorus reduction on early Earth." *Nat Commun* 12, 1535 (2021). https://doi.org/10.1038/s41467-021-21849-2

Higgins, N., & Billings, L. (2017, April 3). "Electric Sand: How Titan's Dunes Got Their Weird Shapes". *Scientific American.* Retrieved May 28, 2023, from https://www.scientificamerican.com/article/electric-sand-how-titans-dunes-got-their-weird-shapes/

Hoffman, Y., Pomarède, D., Tully, R. et al. The dipole repeller. *Nat Astron* 1, 0036 (2017). https://doi.org/10.1038/s41550-016-0036

Hörst SM, et al. "Formation of amino acids and nucleotide bases in a Titan atmosphere simulation experiment." *Astrobiology*. 2012 Sep;12(9):809–17. doi: 10.1089/ast.2011.0623. Epub 2012 Aug 23. PMID: 22917035; PMCID: PMC3444770.

How the earliest life on Earth may have replicated itself. (2018, May 16). MRC Laboratory of Molecular Biology. Retrieved August 18, 2023, from https://www2.mrc-lmb.cam.ac.uk/how-the-earliest-life-on-earth-may-h

Hoyle et al. 1953; Barrow & Tipler 1986: 252–253; Oberhummer et al. 2000; Barnes 2012: sect. 4.7.2

Hubble Focuses on "the Great Attractor". (2013, January 18). NASA. Retrieved May 28, 2023, from https://www.nasa.gov/mission_pages/hubble/science/great-attractor.html

Hughes, Michael F. (7 July 2002). "Arsenic toxicity and potential mechanisms of action". *Toxicology Letters*. 133 (1): 1–16. doi:10.1016/s0378-4274(02)00084-x. ISSN 0378-4274.

Hülse, D., Lau, K. V., van de Velde, S.J. et al. End-Permian marine extinction due to temperature-driven nutrient recycling and euxinia. *Nat. Geosci.* 14, 862–867 (2021). https://doi.org/10.1038/s41561-021-00829-7

In Depth | Titan – NASA Solar System Exploration. (n.d.). NASA Solar System Exploration. Retrieved May 28, 2023, from https://solarsystem.nasa.gov/moons/saturn-moons/titan/in-depth/

J. Dyson, F. (1979). Time without end: Physics and biology in an open universe. *Reviews of Modern Physics*, *51*(3), 451–453. https://www.panspermia.org/revmodphys.51.447.pdf

Jenkins, D. (n.d.). ch6. NASA History Division. Retrieved May 4, 2023, from https://history.nasa.gov/SP-4221/ch6.htm

Kawaguchi Y, et al. "DNA Damage and Survival Time Course of Deinococcal Cell Pellets During 3 Years of Exposure to Outer Space." *Front Microbiol.* 2020 Aug 26;11:2050. doi: 10.3389/fmicb.2020.02050. PMID: 32983036; PMCID: PMC7479814.

Kegerreis, J. A., et al. "Immediate Origin of the Moon as a Post-Impact Satellite." The Astrophysical Journal Letters, vol. 937, no. 2, Oct. 2022, p. L40. Crossref, https://doi.org/10.3847/2041-8213/ac8d96.

Khare, V, Eckert, K. A, "The proofreading 3'→5' exonuclease activity of DNA polymerases: a kinetic barrier to translesion DNA synthesis." (n.d.). *PubMed.* Retrieved May 4, 2023, from https://pubmed.ncbi.nlm.nih.gov/12459442/

Kirshner, R. P. (2002). The Extravagant Universe: Exploding Stars, Dark Energy and the Accelerating Cosmos. Princeton University Press.

Klarreich, E. Callisto's watery secret. *Nature* (2001). https://doi.org/10.1038/news010726-12

Kraan-Korteweg, Renée C., et al. "Discovery of a Supercluster in the Zone of Avoidance in Vela." Monthly Notices of the Royal Astronomical Society: Letters, vol. 466, no. 1, Nov. 2016, pp. L29–33. Crossref, https://doi.org/10.1093/mnrasl/slw229.

Laughlin, S. B., & Sejnowski, T. J. (2003). Communication in neuronal networks. *Science (New York, N.Y.), 301*(5641), 1870–1874. https://doi.org/10.1126/science.1089662

Leblond, L., and Mark W. "Cosmic Necklaces from String Theory." Physical Review D, vol. 75, no. 12, June 2007. Crossref, https://doi.org/10.1103/physrevd.75.123522.

Lee, H. H., Kalhor, R., Goela, N. et al. Terminator-free template-independent enzymatic DNA synthesis for digital information storage. *Nat Commun* 10, 2383 (2019). https://doi.org/10.1038/s41467-019-10258-1

Lee, J. J., & Gramling, C. (2020, September 24). *Life on Earth may have begun in hostile hot springs*. Science News. Retrieved August 18, 2023, from https://www.sciencenews.org/article/life-earth-origins-hostile-hot-springs-microbes

Leitch, C. (2019, February 4). *Insight Into the Earliest Stages of Life on Earth | Cell And Molecular Biology*. Labroots. Retrieved August 18, 2023, from https://www.labroots.com/trending/cell-and-molecular-biology/13965/insight-earliest-stages-life-earth

Lewis, S. (2021, June 29). *Scientists say there's no life on Venus — but Jupiter has potential*. CBS News. Retrieved May 28, 2023, from https://www.cbsnews.com/news/alien-life-venus-jupiter-water-activity-clouds-atmosphere/

Lightning strikes may have been key to origin of life on Earth. (2021, March 17). CBC. Retrieved August 18, 2023, from https://www.cbc.ca/news/science/lightning-origin-of-life-1.5952917

Lin, C., Katla, S. K. & Pérez-Mercader, J. Photochemically induced cyclic morphological dynamics via degradation of autonomously produced, self-assembled polymer vesicles. *Commun Chem* 4, 25 (2021). https://doi.org/10.1038/s42004-021-00464-8

Lincoln et al. Self-Sustained Replication of an RNA Enzyme. *Science*, Jan 8, 2009; doi: 10.1126/science.1167856

Linde, A. (1986). Eternally Existing Self-Reproducing Chaotic Inflationary Universe. *Physics Letters B*, 175(4). https://web.stanford.edu/~alinde/Eternal86.pdf

Linde, A. & Vanchurin, V.. (2009). "How many universes are in the multiverse?" Physical review D: Particles and fields. 81. 10.1103/PhysRevD.81.083525.

Lineweaver, C. H., & Davis, T. M. (2005, March 1). "Misconceptions about the Big Bang." *Scientific American*. Retrieved May 28, 2023, from https://www.scientificamerican.com/article/misconceptions-about-the-2005-03/

Livio, M., Hollowell, D., Weiss, A., Truran, J. W. (27 July 1989). "The anthropic significance of the existence of an excited state of 12C". *Nature*. 340 (6231): 281–84. Bibcode:1989Natur.340..281L. doi:10.1038/340281a0. S2CID 4273737.

Lock, S. J., et al. "The Origin of the Moon Within a Terrestrial Synestia." *Journal of Geophysical Research*: Planets, vol. 123, no. 4, Apr. 2018, pp. 910–51. Portico, Crossref, https://doi.org/10.1002/2017je005333.

Lombard J, López-García P, Moreira D. The early evolution of lipid membranes and the three domains of life. Nat Rev Microbiol. 2012 Jun 11;10(7):507–15. doi: 10.1038/nrmicro2815. PMID: 22683881.

M. Carroll, S., & Chen, J. (n.d.). Spontaneous Inflation and the Origin of the Arrow of Time. *Enrico Fermi Institute, Department of Physics, and Kavli Institute for Cosmological Physics, University of Chicago*, 24–26. https://arxiv.org/pdf/hep-th/0410270.pdf

M. J. Valtonen; G. G. Byrd; M. L. McCall; K. A. Innanen (1993). "A revised history of the Local Group and a generalized method of timing". *Astronomical Journal*. 105: 886–893. Bibcode:1993AJ....105..886V. doi:10.1086/116480.

Mann, A. (2011, November 21). *Search for Alien Life Should Include Exotic Possibilities*. Wired. Retrieved May 28, 2023, from https://www.wired.com/2011/11/alien-life-index/

Markevitch, M., & Werner, N. (2020, February 27). *Record-breaking Explosion by Black Hole Spotted*. NASA. Retrieved May 28, 2023, from https://www.nasa.gov/mission_pages/chandra/news/record-breaking-explosion-by-black-hole-spotted.html

McCook, G. P., & Sion, E. M. (1999). A Catalogue of Spectroscopically Identified White Dwarfs. *The Astrophysical Journal Supplement Series*. 121 (1): 1–130.

McKay, C. P., Smith, H. D. (2005). "Possibilities for methanogenic life in liquid methane on the surface of Titan". *Icarus*. 178 (1): 274–276.

Miret-Roig, N., Bouy, H., Raymond, S. N. et al. A rich population of free-floating planets in the Upper Scorpius young stellar association. *Nat Astron* 6, 89–97 (2022). https://doi.org/10.1038/s41550-021-01513-x

Mullen, L. (2010, May 31). "Mars was Wet, but was it Warm?" *Phys.org*. Retrieved August 18, 2023, from https://phys.org/news/2010-05-mars.html

Mysterious Cosmic 'Dark Flow' Tracked Deeper into Universe. (2010, October 3). NASA. Retrieved August 18, 2023, from https://www.nasa.gov/centers/goddard/news/releases/2010/10-023.html

Mystery of Universe's Expansion Rate Widens With New Hubble Data. (2019, April 25). NASA. Retrieved May 28, 2023, from https://www.nasa.gov/feature/goddard/2019/mystery-of-the-universe-s-expansion-rate-widens-with-new-hubble-data

N. Chandra Wickramasinghe, Fred Hoyle (1981). *Evolution from Space*. London: J.M. Dent & Sons.

Nakayama, Y., & Kawai, S. (2016). "Reheating of the Universe as holographic thermalization." *ScienceDirect*, 759, 546–549. https://www.sciencedirect.com/science/article/pii/S0370269316302726

New Study of Uranus' Large Moons Shows 4 May Hold Water. (2023, May 4). NASA. Retrieved May 28, 2023, from https://www.nasa.gov/feature/jpl/new-study-of-uranus-large-moons-shows-4-may-hold-water

Norby, D. (2006, January 1). "How close can stars get to each other in galaxy cores?" *Astronomy*. Retrieved March 18, 2023, from https://astronomy.com/magazine/ask-astro/2006/01/how-close-can-stars-get-to-each-other-in-galaxy-cores

O'Malley-James, Jack T., Kaltenegger, L. (July 2017). "UV surface habitability of the TRAPPIST-1 system". *Monthly Notices of the Royal Astronomical Society: Letters.* 469 (1): L26–L30. doi:10.1093/mnrasl/slx047.

Ocean of magma blasted into space may explain how the moon formed. (2019, April 30). ZME Science. Retrieved May 28, 2023, from https://www.zmescience.com/space/ocean-magma-moon-formation-04232/

Ocean on Saturn Moon Could be as Salty as the Dead Sea. (2014, July 2). Jet Propulsion Laboratory. Retrieved May 28, 2023, from https://www.jpl.nasa.gov/news/ocean-on-saturn-moon-could-be-as-salty-as-the-dead-sea

Ortiz, J. L., et al. "The Size, Shape, Density and Ring of the Dwarf Planet Haumea from a Stellar Occultation." Nature, vol. 550, no. 7675, Oct. 2017, pp. 219–23. Crossref, https://doi.org/10.1038/nature24051.

Overview | Kuiper Belt – NASA Solar System Exploration. (n.d.). NASA Solar System Exploration. Retrieved August 18, 2023, from https://solarsystem.nasa.gov/solar-system/kuiper-belt/overview/

Oxygen-Free, Methane-Based Life Forms Could Exist on Titan, Say Scientists. (2015, February 28). Sci.News. Retrieved May 4, 2023, from https://www.sci.news/space/science-azotosome-oxygen-free-methane-based-life-forms-titan-02549.html

Page, Don. (1994). Information Loss in Black Holes and/or Conscious Beings? *CIAR Cosmology Program, Institute for Theoretical Physics*, 7–8. https://arxiv.org/pdf/hep-th/9411193.pdf

Pearce, Ben K. D., et al. "Toward RNA Life on Early Earth: From Atmospheric HCN to Biomolecule Production in Warm Little Ponds." The Astrophysical Journal, vol. 932, no. 1, June 2022, p. 9. Crossref, https://doi.org/10.3847/1538-4357/ac47a1.

Peebles, P. J. E., & Ratra, B. (2003). The cosmological constant and dark energy. *Reviews of Modern Physics*. 75 (2): 559–606. https://arxiv.org/pdf/astro-ph/0207347.pdf

Petit, Jean-Marc; Morbidelli, Alessandro (2001). "The Primordial Excitation and Clearing of the Asteroid Belt" (PDF). *Icarus*. 153 (2): 338–347. Bibcode:2001Icar..153..338P. doi:10.1006/icar.2001.6702. Archived from the original (PDF) on 2007-02-21. Retrieved 2006-11-19.

Physicists Calculate Number of Universes in the Multiverse. (2009, October 15). MIT Technology Review. Retrieved August 18, 2023, from https://www.technologyreview.com/2009/10/15/123729/physicists-calculate-number-of-universes-in-the-multiverse/

Pidcock, R. (2016, August 24). *Scientists clarify starting point for human-caused climate change*. Carbon Brief. Retrieved March 25, 2023, from https://www.carbonbrief.org/scientists-clarify-starting-point-for-human-caused-climate-change/

Piovesan A., Pelleri M. C., Antonaros F., Strippoli P., Caracausi M., Vitale L. On the length, weight and GC content of the human genome. BMC Res Notes. 2019 Feb 27;12(1):106. doi: 10.1186/s13104-019-4137-z. PMID: 30813969; PMCID: PMC6391780.

Pitjeva, E. V. (2018). "Masses of the Main Asteroid Belt and the Kuiper Belt from the Motions of Planets and Spacecraft". *Solar System Research*. 44 (8–9): 554–566. arXiv:1811.05191.

Preston B. D., Albertson T. M., Herr A. J. DNA replication fidelity and cancer. Semin Cancer Biol. 2010 Oct;20(5):281–93. doi: 10.1016/j.semcancer.2010.10.009. Epub 2010 Oct 15. PMID: 20951805; PMCID: PMC2993855.

Rakic P. Evolution of the neocortex: a perspective from developmental biology. Nat Rev Neurosci. 2009 Oct;10(10):724–35. doi: 10.1038/nrn2719. PMID: 19763105; PMCID: PMC2913577.

Riess, Adam G., et al. (1998). Observational Evidence from Supernovae for an Accelerating Universe and a Cosmological Constant. *The Astronomical Journal*. 116 (3): 1009–1038. https://arxiv.org/pdf/astro-ph/9805201.pdf

Robertson M. P., Joyce G. F. Highly efficient self-replicating RNA enzymes. Chem Biol. 2014 Feb 20;21(2):238–45. doi: 10.1016/j.chembiol.2013.12.004. Epub 2014 Jan 2. PMID: 24388759; PMCID: PMC3943892.

Rommel, F. L., Braga-Ribas, F., Desmars, J., et al. (December 2020). "Stellar occultations enable milliarcsecond astrometry for Trans-Neptunian objects and Centaurs". *Astronomy & Astrophysics*. 644: 15. arXiv:2010.12708. Bibcode:2020A&A...644A..40R. doi:10.1051/0004-6361/202039054. S2CID 225070222. A40.

Sagan, C. (2000). Carl Sagan's Cosmic Connection: an Extraterrestrial Perspective (2nd ed.). Cambridge U.P. p. 46.

Sara Seager, Janusz J. Petkowski, Peter Gao, William Bains, Noelle C. Bryan, Sukrit Ranjan, and Jane Greaves. "The Venusian Lower Atmosphere Haze as a Depot for Desiccated Microbial Life: A Proposed Life Cycle for Persistence of the Venusian Aerial Biosphere." *Astrobiology*. Oct 2021. 1206–1223. http://doi.org/10.1089/ast.2020.2244

Sauers, E. (2023, April 18). *Webb telescope sees galaxy collision brighter than 1 trillion suns*. Mashable. Retrieved May 28, 2023, from https://mashable.com/article/james-webb-space-telescope-spiral-galaxy-merger

Schirber, M. (2006, June 9). *How Life Began: New Research Suggests Simple Approach*. Live Science. Retrieved May 28, 2023, from https://www.livescience.com/10531-life-began-research-suggests-simple-approach.html

Schneider, J. (2012, February 12). *Interactive Extra-solar Planets Catalog*. The Extrasolar Planets Encyclopedia. Retrieved March 18, 2023, from http://exoplanet.eu/catalog/

Schulze, D. (2020, June 11). Silicon-Based Life, That Staple of Science Fiction, May Not Be Likely After All. Smithsonian Magazine. Retrieved May 4, 2023, from https://www.smithsonianmag.com/air-space-magazine/silicon-based-life-staple-science-fiction-may-not-be-likely-after-all-180975083/

Science: The Fleeting Flesh - TIME. (n.d.). Videos Index on TIME. com. Retrieved May 4, 2023, from https://content.time.com/time/subscriber/article/0,33009,936455,00.html

Scoles, S. (2019, August 5). *The Virgo Supercluster: Our 100,000 closest galaxies | Astronomy.com*. Astronomy Magazine. Retrieved May 28, 2023, from https://www.astronomy.com/science/the-virgo-supercluster-our-100000-closest-galaxies/

Sedna (2003 VB12). (n.d.). CalTech GPS. Retrieved August 18, 2023, from https://web.gps.caltech.edu/~mbrown/sedna/

Shapiro, R. (2007, September 5). *Robert Shapiro—LIFE: WHAT A CONCEPT!* Edge.org. Retrieved June 7, 2023, from https://www.edge.org/conversation/robert_shapiro-robert-shapiro%E2%80%94life-what-a-concept

Sholtis, S. (2019, January 31). *Membraneless protocells could provide clues to formation of early life*. Penn State. Retrieved August 18, 2023, from https://www.psu.edu/news/research/story/membrane-less-protocells-could-provide-clues-formation-early-life/

Short-Term Energy Outlook. (n.d.). Short-Term Energy Outlook - U.S. Energy Information Administration (EIA). Retrieved May 4, 2023, from https://www.eia.gov/outlooks/steo/report/global_oil.php

Siegel, E. (2022, January 17). Hoiw many planets are there in the Universe? Big Think. Retrieved May 4, 2023, from https://bigthink.com/starts-with-a-bang/planets-universe/

Simon J. Lock, Sarah T. Stewart, Michail I. Petaev, Zoë M. Leinhardt, Mia T. Mace, Stein B. Jacobsen, Matija Ćuk. The origin of the Moon within a terrestrial synestia. *Journal of Geophysical Research: Planets*, 2018; DOI: 10.1002/2017JE005333

Sithamparam M., Satthiyasilan N., Chen C., Jia T. Z., Chandru K. A material-based panspermia hypothesis: The potential of polymer gels and membraneless droplets. Biopolymers. 2022 May;113(5):e23486. doi: 10.1002/bip.23486. Epub 2022 Feb 11. PMID: 35148427.

Spacek, Jan. (2021). Organic Carbon Cycle in the Atmosphere of Venus.

Steele, B. (1999, November 12). *It's the 25th anniversary of Earth's first attempt to phone E.T.* Cornell Chronicle. Retrieved April 6, 2023, from https://news.cornell.edu/stories/1999/11/25th-anniversary-first-attempt-phone-et-0

Stevenson, D. Life-sustaining planets in interstellar space?. *Nature* 400, 32 (1999). https://doi.org/10.1038/21811

Stewart, G. (2012, February 23). "Researchers Say Galaxy May Swarm with Nomad Planets" | *SLAC*... SLAC National Accelerator Laboratory. Retrieved May 28, 2023, from https://www6.slac.stanford.edu/news/2012-02-23-researchers-say-galaxy-may-swarm-nomad-planets

Strickland, A. (2019, September 20). "Venus was potentially habitable until a mysterious event happened." CNN. Retrieved May 28, 2023, from https://edition.cnn.com/2019/09/20/world/venus-habitability-scn/index.html

Strigari, Louis E., et al. "Nomads of the Galaxy." *Monthly Notices of the Royal Astronomical Society*, vol. 423, no. 2, May 2012, pp. 1856–65. Crossref, https://doi.org/10.1111/j.1365-2966.2012.21009.x.

Strobel, Darrell. (2010). Molecular hydrogen in Titan's atmosphere: Implications of the measured tropospheric and thermospheric mole fractions. Icarus. 208. 878–886. 10.1016/j.icarus.2010.03.003.

Su M., Ling Y., Yu J., Wu J., Xiao J. Small proteins: untapped area of potential biological importance. Front Genet. 2013 Dec 16;4:286. doi: 10.3389/fgene.2013.00286. PMID: 24379829; PMCID: PMC3864261.

Takahiro Sudoh et al. "Testing anthropic reasoning for the cosmological constant with a realistic galaxy formation model." *Monthly Notices of the Royal Astronomical Society*, Volume 464, Issue 2, January 2017, Pages 1563–1568, https://doi.org/10.1093/mnras/stw2401

Tegmark, M. (2003). Parallel Universes. *Science and Ultimate Reality: From Quantum to Cosmos*, 1–5. https://space.mit.edu/home/tegmark/multiverse.pdf

Than, K. (2007, August 14). *Hot Gas in Space Mimics Life*. Space.com. Retrieved August 18, 2023, from https://www.space.com/4219-hot-gas-space-mimics-life.html

The electric sands of Titan: The grains that cover Saturn's moon act like clingy packing peanuts. (2017, March 27). Phys.org. Retrieved May 28, 2023, from https://phys.org/news/2017-03-electric-sands-titan-grains-saturn.html

The Microlensing Observations in Astrophysics (MOA) Collaboration. "The Optical Gravitational Lensing Experiment (OGLE) Collaboration. Unbound or distant planetary mass population detected by gravitational microlensing." *Nature* 473, 349–352 (2011). https://doi.org/10.1038/nature10092

The Price of War: Russia's War on Ukraine Costs $8.9T at Five-Months. (2022, August 4). C.D. Howe Institute. Retrieved May 4, 2023, from https://www.cdhowe.org/media-release/price-war-russias-war-ukraine-costs-89t-five-months

The Solar System Beyond the Orbit of Neptune V = 2π r R. (n.d.). Space Math @ NASA. Retrieved August 18, 2023, from https://spacemath.gsfc.nasa.gov/weekly/10Page64.pdf

Titan's Underground Ocean | Science Mission Directorate. (2012, June 28). NASA Science. Retrieved May 28, 2023, from https://science.nasa.gov/science-news/science-at-nasa/2012/28jun_titanocean

Toll, T. (2016, July 25). *Of Gluons and Fireflies.* Physics. Retrieved April 20, 2023, from https://physics.aps.org/articles/v9/82

Trosper, J. (n.d.). *Dark Flow: A Mysterious Force From Outside of our Local Universe.* Futurism. Retrieved August 18, 2023, from https://futurism.com/dark-flow

Tsytovich, V. N., et al. (2007). "From plasma crystals and helical structures towards inorganic living matter." *New Journal of Physics*, 9(8), 263. doi:101088/1367-2630/9/8/263

Tucker, I. (2011, August 27). *Lee Cronin: 'Aliens could be made from iron'.* The Guardian. Retrieved May 28, 2023, from https://www.theguardian.com/technology/2011/aug/28/aliens-iron-evolution-lee-cronin

University of Copenhagen - The Faculty of Health and Medical Sciences. "Mars was once covered by 300-meter deep oceans, study shows." ScienceDaily. ScienceDaily, 17 November 2022. www.sciencedaily.com/releases/2022/11/221117102806.htm.

Unravelling the Origin of Life. (2022, February 14). NCBS News. Retrieved August 18, 2023, from https://news.ncbs.res.in/research-explained/unravelling-origin-life

Wall, M. (2017, June 8). *Comets May Have Delivered Many of Life's Building Blocks to Early Earth.* Space.com. Retrieved May 28, 2023, from https://www.space.com/37135-comets-life-building-blocks-earth-rosetta.html

Way, M. J., et al. "Was Venus the First Habitable World of Our Solar System?" Geophysical Research Letters, vol. 43, no. 16, Aug. 2016, pp. 8376–83. Portico, Crossref, https://doi.org/10.1002/2016gl069790.

Webb Captures the Spectacular Galactic Merger Arp 220. (2023, April 17). Webb Space Telescope. Retrieved August 18, 2023, from https://webbtelescope.org/contents/news-releases/2023/news-2023-116.html

Weinberg 1987; Barnes 2012: sect. 4.6; Schellekens 2013: sect. 3

Weissman, P. R. (n.d.). *The mass of the Oort cloud*. NASA/ADS. Retrieved August 18, 2023, from https://ui.adsabs.harvard.edu/abs/1983A%26A...118...90W/abstract

Welsh, T. (2015, June 26). It feels instantaneous, but how long does it really take to think a thought? The Conversation. Retrieved May 4, 2023, from https://theconversation.com/it-feels-instantaneous-but-how-long-does-it-really-take-to-think-a-thought-42392

Wesson, Paul S. "Panspermia, Past and Present: Astrophysical and Biophysical Conditions for the Dissemination of Life in Space." Space Science Reviews, vol. 156, no. 1–4, July 2010, pp. 239–52. Crossref, https://doi.org/10.1007/s11214-010-9671-x.

Williams, M. (2021, March 15). *About 7 interstellar objects pass through the inner solar system every year, study estimates*. Phys.org. Retrieved May 28, 2023, from https://phys.org/news/2021-03-interstellar-solar-year.html

WMAP CMB Fluctuations. (2014, August 20). Wilkinson Microwave Anisotropy Probe. Retrieved May 4, 2023, from https://wmap.gsfc.nasa.gov/universe/bb_cosmo_fluct.html

WMAP- Shape of the Universe. (2014, January 24). Wilkinson Microwave Anisotropy Probe. Retrieved August 18, 2023, from https://map.gsfc.nasa.gov/universe/uni_shape.html

WMAP- Shape of the Universe. (2014, January 24). Wilkinson Microwave Anisotropy Probe. Retrieved May 28, 2023, from https://map.gsfc.nasa.gov/universe/uni_shape.html

Yates, Jack S., et al. "Atmospheric Habitable Zones in Y Dwarf Atmospheres." The Astrophysical Journal, vol. 836, no. 2, Feb. 2017, p. 184. Crossref, https://doi.org/10.3847/1538-4357/836/2/184.

Young, K. (2006, June 6). *Andromeda galaxy hosts a trillion stars*. New Scientist. Retrieved August 18, 2023, from https://www.newscientist.com/article/dn9282-andromeda-galaxy-hosts-a-trillion-stars/

ABOUT THE AUTHOR

Nathan Hellner-Mestelman is an avid writer and science communicator. A contributor to *Sky's Up* magazine and the former *SkyNews* magazine, he enjoys sharing our place in the universe with the public. As a member of the Royal Astronomical Society of Canada, he does outreach at the Dominion Astrophysical Observatory. His work has been featured in the *Lonely Planet Anthology*, *Physics World Magazine*, and *Math Horizons*. His recent award-winning film, *Universe Versus You*, was screened at film festivals internationally. He currently lives in British Columbia, Canada, with his two cats and family.